TOP FLYTE

Sir Raymond Flyte is the epitome of the successful millionaire — dapper, witty, shrewd and ruthless. With an imminent takeover, he is set to become one of the most powerful men in British industry. No whiff of scandal has ever breathed near Raymond Flyte — until up-and-coming journalist Tony Roberts starts to uncover the sordid truth behind Flyte and his empire. Some men will stoop too low in their struggle for success. 'Anything goes' is the saying, and anything does — for Raymond Flyte.

LEO METCALFE

TOP
FLYTE

Complete and Unabridged

LINFORD
Leicester

LP
METCALF

First published in Great Britain in 1987

First Linford Edition
published 2000

British Library CIP Data

Metcalfe, Leo
    Top flyte.—Large print ed.—
    Linford mystery library
    1. Detective and mystery stories
    2. Large type books
    I. Title
    823.9′14 [F]

    ISBN 0–7089–5741–2

Published by
F. A. Thorpe (Publishing)
Anstey, Leicestershire

Set by Words & Graphics Ltd.
Anstey, Leicestershire
Printed and bound in Great Britain by
T. J. International Ltd., Padstow, Cornwall

This book is printed on acid-free paper

FOR MARION

The Boardroom

Sir Raymond Flyte KBE, sat in his chair, looking along the polished mahogany table. Heavy crystal chandeliers hung down, illuminating the scene. The windows were covered by long floor-to-ceiling velvet curtains. The room was pleasantly warm but not oppressive as the air filtered through the conditioning system.

Six men sat at the table, three on each side. At the far end, well removed but within hearing distance, sat a well-groomed secretary. Her shorthand pad was in front of her and close by stood a taperecorder with its wheels turning, registering everything that was being said.

Sir Raymond said, 'All right, Susan, that covers it.' He looked at his watch and added, 'It's nearly seven now. Get those minutes typed up straight away. I'll be going to my club in Knightsbridge shortly. When you've finished, phone me there and I'll come back to sign them. Two copies only, and no spares — both to go into my safe. Don't forget to destroy the tape and shred your shorthand notes.'

She rose from the table, lifting the book and the tape-recorder. Her feet made no sound on the deep pile carpet as she crossed the room. As the door closed softly behind her, Sir Raymond Flyte rose to his feet, pushing back his chair. He rested his hands on the table, and leaned forward in one of his typically aggressive poses. His firm chin jutted out and he scanned the men seated in front of him.

'Gentlemen, there is nothing further we can do tonight. You have been involved in the close discussions over the past months whereby Flyte Enterprises will acquire a fifty-one per cent shareholding in the Felix Industrial Group. We have been lucky that nothing of our talks has leaked out to the press or other organisations. You know the hard bargaining that has gone on behind closed doors and at hidden meetings. You know the difficulties that have had to be overcome with the institutional shareholder in particular, and how they are now on our side.

'Tomorrow we will be at the offices of Felix Industries to sign the formal Scheme of Arrangement and to send out the press releases on what has been agreed. We are nearly there, gentlemen. Everything has been thought out and taken care of — but once the news becomes public, it will make the headlines. There are now only the normal public formalities to be completed. Then we shall be home and dry. That is probably going to take another two months — if that.

'In the meantime, all of us here must keep a low profile on our personal and public lives. When you are hounded for comment by the news media, financial pundits and your future colleagues at Felix Industries, you must emphasise again and again that, although we will be acquiring a majority shareholding, it is *not* — I repeat *not* — a takeover. It is the merger of business interests. Let us say a marriage.'

He raised himself, and suddenly his

face changed to the impish-eyed smiling Raymond Flyte of his press photographs.

'Remember though, whenever there is a marriage — someone is bound to get fucked.'

1

The plane got me into Heathrow about midnight and I went straight to my Park Lane hotel and had a good night's sleep.

In the morning, I enjoyed a full English breakfast and walked from the hotel in the direction of Fleet Street, relishing the rain and the sights and smells of London. There was an acute contrast to the open deserts and baked earth of the Middle East, not to mention the squalid backstreets of many a town and city there. In the past three years I had been back to London only twice, although I had attended meetings and conferences in other parts of Europe. As I approached Piccadilly Circus, I looked at my watch and flagged down a taxi. Ten minutes later, I was in our Head Office building in the heart of London's newspaper world.

I walked through the newspaper office's

main press room with what seemed like hundreds of desks, ringing telephones and clacking typewriters. There was the usual orderly disorder, incomprehensible to those outside the world of newspapers. Although I had once worked in this room there now seemed hardly anyone I knew.

I recognised the familiar faces in the glass cubicled offices at the end, though. I had a few words with most of them before I mounted the stairs to the office of Bill Travis, the Foreign News Editor. It was to his desk that my reports over the past three years had been sent. It was over his telephone that I received any special instructions, and it was over his telephone that I spoke to him initially when I had some very urgent news to impart. I tapped on his door and went in. He was, as usual, talking on the telephone. He seemed to live on it, and had a battery of machines in different colours across his desk. Two men I didn't recognise sat in front of him and they turned as I walked in. The air was blue from cigarette smoke, which even the whirring fan in the grimy window couldn't clear.

Bill said into the phone, 'Just a minute,' and he capped his hand over the telephone mouthpiece.

'Welcome home, Tony — talk to you in a minute. David, Jack, this is Tony Roberts — Middle East. Say hullo until I get this twit off the line.'

He went on with his conversation while I talked to David and Jack, who I gathered were just on their way to Hong Kong and then to China. Eventually Bill slammed down the receiver.

'Bollocks,' he said. 'That man of ours in Paris really is a piss artist — still we could do worse.'

He came round the desk and seemed to tower over me as he gripped my hand. I am nearly six feet tall and no lightweight but Bill was a great bear of a man. Fiftyish, greying hair, almost never without a cigarette. He turned to David and Jack, and said:

'If you want examples of good, clear, precise and informed reporting, you could do worse than spend the afternoon reading what this young fellow has sent back over the past three years.' Glancing back towards me, he winked and said, 'Tony, I'm slightly tied up at the moment with these two aspiring bright sparks, but let's have lunch together. Book a table at Simpsons for one o'clock — meet you in the downstairs bar? Meanwhile, go and talk to accounts about your salary arrangements and expenses. I'm sure they'll be delighted to see you.'

He turned away and continued his conversation as if I hadn't intruded. I made my peace with the accounts department and booked the table for lunch. The rain had stopped when I left the building and I walked slowly along Fleet Street and down the Strand.

It was 1.15 when Bill entered the downstairs bar. I drained my pint of bitter and ordered two more. Bill's rule of lunchtime drinking was well known. A pint before the meal and one with it and then stop. He wasn't one of the newspaper soaks of popular belief. We talked about the handover

8

to the new correspondent who was to be based in Saudi and then went up to the dining-room. We talked general newspaper 'shop' but when we got to the coffee stage, Bill said:

'Now, Tony, I have news for you. The Old Man has been very impressed with your stuff from the Middle East and seems to think you're a bright boy. I, of course, have done my best to disillusion him,' he added with a twinkle in his eye. 'But you know the Old Man. Once he gets an idea into his head, nobody can dislodge it. So I bow to the inevitable and am happy to go along with him. Sometimes, anyway. He seems to think, and on this one I agree, that, after your leave, you should cut your teeth on Africa. We've had John Stevens out there for a long time and he's been keeping a fatherly eye on the other bods we have there — plus the stringers that work for him. In the last six months, though, his health has been poor and things have been slipping a bit. I'm going to bring him home for a spell and he can work for me here until we get his bugs sorted out. Then we'll decide on where he should go next.

'Don't worry, he won't topple you out of Africa unless you make a balls of it. If we thought that might happen, you wouldn't be going. Bigger responsibility, more money, bigger expense account to fiddle, house, garden and servants all thrown in. I thought you should be based in Zimbabwe — there's a lot happening down that way. It's a lovely country, have you ever been there?'

'No,' I said. 'Only to parts of North Africa — Egypt, Ethiopia, Libya and the Sudan.'

'That's right. I remember now. You had to go there to cover a few times for us. Well, take my word for it, Zimbabwe has something like an English climate without the rain and snow pissing down half the time, and minus the miles of sweet bugger-all except sand. You'll be going all over Africa but it's good to have a pleasant, firm base to work from.' He stopped suddenly, looking at me. 'You don't seem brimming over with enthusiasm at your promotion. What's up?'

'Bill, I don't know how to tell you,' I began.

'Tell me what, for Christ's sake? You haven't put some Arab princess in the pudding club, have you? A thing like that could start a Third World War.'

'It isn't as simple as that.' When he was about to speak again, I added: 'Please give me the chance to explain.'

He lit another cigarette took a deep gulp of smoke and blew it out. He poured himself some more coffee and then said, 'Go on then, I'm listening. Explain.'

I felt like asking him for a cigarette but I'd given them up ten years ago. I took a deep breath and began:

'It's like this. My time in the Middle East has given me a great chance to think about things. The great expansion schemes were under way there long before I arrived. With the almost unlimited oil wealth, the Arabs have rapidly sprung forward into the twentieth century — some would say the twenty-first. Their money can buy anything. New towns. New cities. New airports. New hospitals. New anything they want. All the industrialised nations of the world are clamouring to sell them every sort of scheme under the sun, and in many cases succeeding. Fifty years ago the Arab countries had nothing, and now in effect, they control the economy of the world because of their oil and their huge investment muscle. All right, they've learnt how to use their money and have moved from being street traders to sophisticated entrepreneurs with university degrees. My point is, though, that they haven't earned their money. It was under the ground and would have stayed there if we hadn't come along with our know-how and our technology and dug it up for them. The industrial nations benefit because they can buy the oil even at the inflated prices and charge more for their goods and services to cover the cost. While this is going on the other half of the world slips further back into even deeper stagnation and starvation. Not only have I seen this almost obscene Arab wealth but

I've also seen the jackals from the already wealthy industrialised nations crawling for a bigger share of the Arab cake. You've seen my confidential reports on the bribes for contracts and the millions of pounds that have been changing hands to buy them. Some of our most distinguished citizens — so called — have been involved. Across the Red Sea in Ethiopia tens of thousands of people are starving to death and we cheer if we see an Oxfam truck full of dried milk with the Union Jack on the side. How much food would a million-pound bribe buy for starving people? That in a nutshell is what is bugging me and the trouble is, I don't know the answer.'

Bill stubbed his cigarette out and promptly lit another one. He blew out the smoke between clenched teeth. Then he said quietly:

'Do you think that you've told me anything that I, and a hell of a lot of other people, don't know? I'm fifty-two and I've been behind my present desk for the past seven years. The previous twenty years I spent doing what you have been doing for the past three. Going back over those twenty-seven years, do you think that I wasn't appalled at what I saw in my travels? Do you think I don't care? To be a good journalist you've got to care, otherwise you can't report objectively. Our job is to tell people what is going on, let them make their minds up for themselves and hope the politicians will do something about it. If you want to try to change the world, then go in for politics and see how far you'll get. You won't get anywhere. Stick to what you're good at — objective reporting and at least hope that things will change. They have, you know, over the last hundred years, and they no doubt will over the next hundred — but it's a slow process.'

I looked down at my clasped hands on the table. 'What about all the detailed reports I sent you, backed up with proof about the corruption in high places over Middle East government contracts? You didn't publish any of them. Why was that?'

'You use the word 'corruption' to describe what some people might regard as the traditional business practices of other countries. When we Brits had an Empire and controlled things, we largely stamped out corruption in areas we controlled, even in parts of the world where sweetening the middleman had been common business practice for centuries before we came onto the scene. When we left, everything just reverted to normal. Now we have, like everyone else, to join in the game. If we filled our columns exposing, if you can call it that, what really goes on in the Middle East, and elsewhere too, all that would happen is that the British press and other media would be kicked out. Then there would be no British media reporting at all. We'd lose any hope of any government contracts overseas and perhaps stir up an international situation. Look what happened over the showing of that TV film *Death of a Princess*. It was political dynamite. Cut off trade links with the Middle East and God knows how many extra people will join the dole queues here. Think about that.'

'So the end justifies the means or — if

you can't beat them join them,' I said, rather irritably.

Bill replied, 'That is the biggest load of crap I've heard from you in a long time. You sound like a sixth-form debating society. I'm beginning to wonder about you. Have you gone Commie all of a sudden? You're beginning to sound like it.'

He glanced at his watch.

'Now listen to me, Tony. At your stage in the game I often felt as you do now, but I realised that I had to face up to things as they were and not as I would like them to be. You've just got back after three years and you need time to orientate. You've got three months' leave due to you and I think you need it. Come into the office any time you like but I suggest you go away and think things over.' As he rose to his feet he added: 'And for talking to you like a Dutch uncle, you can bloody well pay the bill.'

He strode out of the room, lighting another cigarette. I ordered myself a whisky and soda, going over our conversation in my mind. I came to the conclusion that I hadn't explained things very well.

* * *

The following day I went up to my parents' home in a small Midlands country town. They lived in a cobbled street of preserved Elizabethan houses under the shelter of the castle wall. Real picture-postcard stuff. My mother met the train at the nearby station and the obvious delight at our reunion was quite mutual. I had always got on well with my parents and looked upon them as older-generation friends. My father was a local bank manager who, had he been more ambitious, could no doubt have reached the higher echelons of banking, but he let it be known, early in his career, that he wanted to stay in his local area. I suppose, in a way, I envied his contentment: both he and my mother were absorbed in one another and the happenings of the local community.

My father made a point of getting home early that evening and we sat at the kitchen table with a bottle of whisky, while my mother prepared the evening meal. They listened to my comments about the Arab countries I'd visited since I'd last seen them. They brought me up to date on all the local gossip of friends and acquaintances. I skated vaguely over the question of what I'd be doing next and they didn't press me. They were happy to have me home and I was happy to be there.

Over the next ten days, I visited old school chums, family friends, and the Midland City newspaper office where I'd started as a young journalist. At my father's request I even gave a talk at the local Rotary Club luncheon.

I met a friend I'd been at school with and who had a sailing boat on the south coast. He had suggested I borrowed it for a week while a spell of good weather was with us. I had sailed a lot with him in the past so he knew that I was unlikely to do it any harm. While I was enjoying this seafaring excursion I arranged to meet another friend, now living in one of the sailing towns on the

Solent. We decided to meet one evening in the local yacht club.

I tied up alongside the visitors' pontoon late one afternoon, secured the boat and tidied things up, including myself before walking to the yacht club, enjoying the warm evening.

Robin McMullen was in the bar with his wife, Kathie, to give me the 'long lost friend treatment' accompanied by the rapid sinking of a few pints of beer.

Kathie, always one to enjoy a good get-together, joined in the general fun but her expression became more serious as she glanced at her watch and said:

'A friend of ours is coming to join us for dinner, she should be here soon.' She looked rather anxiously about. 'I think you're going to get on well. She's great fun normally but has been having rather a hard time just lately and needs cheering up, so we're relying on you. She's on leave from the Middle East, so you should have something in common. She's a doctor out there.'

'And what's her problem?' I asked flippantly. 'Broken love affair?'

'I wish it was as simple as that. Her father was a local doctor here — a lovely man. He died about three years ago and his wife died recently. There have been all sorts of rumours because she apparently took too many sleeping pills or something — but it's all been quietly hushed up, whatever it was. They'd lost all their money or something and now Pat, — that's the daughter, Pat Sheriden — has come home to sort things out. So,' she said, brightening her mood, 'we want some cheery conversation out of you tonight, Tony Roberts.'

We ordered some more drinks and then Pat Sheriden walked into the bar. She was small and slim with immaculately groomed red hair. Her blue eyes surveyed the room then lit up with a smile as she saw us. Her lightly tanned face accentuated the colour of her eyes and I gauged her to be in her late twenties. The introductions were made, more drinks were consumed.

Over dinner we talked of the Middle East, the newspaper world, and our hilarious university days. We were all happy and relaxed and I caught a look from Robin and Kathie, which said, 'Well done, mate'. At about ten o'clock Kathie glanced at her watch and said they'd got to be off to relieve the babysitter, and together they left us with instructions for me to telephone them in the morning.

When Pat had finished her coffee, I settled the bill and we drove back to the marina in her car. I suggested she came on board for a nightcap, and she willingly agreed. She was good company and easy to talk to, and I felt more than disappointment when she refused my offer to come sailing the next day explaining that she was tied up with all sorts of family problems. As a compromise we exchanged addresses and phone numbers and I promised to contact her again.

I sailed in the Solent for the next two days, enjoying both the sun and solitude, but most of the time I found myself thinking of Pat Sheriden.

* * *

When I got home I found a message to phone her and went straight through to my father's study and dialled the number. She answered almost immediately and, after chatting about my last couple of days' sailing, she said:

'Tony, I want to ask your help over something. I don't know if Robin and Kathie told you, but both my father and my mother died recently and left an awful financial mess. I'm not sure what I'm going to do but I feel the need to talk to someone outside the family. Somebody who knows about things — or at least can find out.'

'Is this to do with the financial side?' I asked.

'Yes. It really is a mess and everyone is just sitting back complacently and making trite remarks in a philosophical way about the ways of the world. It's all too difficult to explain over the telephone.' She paused. 'Is there any chance that we could meet? I know it's a hell of a lot to ask from someone you've only met briefly but I have a feeling you might be able to help.'

'Of course,' I replied, delighted at the thought. 'Would you like me to come down to you?'

'No. Not here. Somehow it's too close to things. I could drive up to you, though, tomorrow morning and be with you about lunchtime.'

I paused to consider. 'I don't think that would be the best idea, for a similar reason.' It might not be easy to talk confidentially with my father in the next room. I asked, 'Can you give me a clue what it's all about?'

'As I've said, it's very difficult over the telephone. It involves a man called Raymond Flyte — Sir Raymond Flyte to be precise. Have you heard of him?'

'Only vaguely. I know that he's some sort of commercial empire-builder but I've never been involved with the City and the commercial end of things — but wait a minute. It would be easy for me to find out.'

'That's what I hoped you'd say.'

'Let me think,' I said. 'How would it be if we met in London tomorrow for lunch and you can fill me in on the background? I can then go and have a talk with our City boys if I feel it would help.'

'That would be marvellous. Are you sure you don't mind?'

'I'd be delighted. What about one o'clock in the entrance lounge of the Grosvenor House Hotel?'

'Fine. I'll see you tomorrow.'

I dialled the London number of my newspaper and was put through to the cuttings library. There was always someone on duty, day and night. I explained who I was and that I wanted everything pulled out for me that they'd got on Sir Raymond Flyte. I told them I'd be in the following afternoon.

As I walked through to join my father, he lowered his newspaper and asked, 'Did I hear you mention the name of Raymond Flyte?'

'That's right,' I said, suddenly interested. 'Do you know anything about him?'

'Only what I read in the press and see on television. He's quite a character, I believe. Made a fortune for himself and a lot of other people, too. We could do with a lot more men like him — lots of drive and initiative. One of the old merchant-adventurer types — a real goer.'

★ ★ ★

I walked into the foyer of the Grosvenor House Hotel at 12.40 the next day and booked myself a room. From the far end of the lounge I caught sight of Pat Sheriden, seated in a comfortable armchair. As I walked over to her, I glanced at my watch. She must have seen it for, as I came up, she said, smiling:

'It's all right. I'm the early bird. My train got in at twelve and having dragged you up here, I thought the least I could do was to be on time. Anyway it's very pleasant sitting here watching the world go by.' She levelled her blue eyes at me and I thought how lovely she looked. I seated myself in an armchair beside her and ordered some drinks.

'I hope you don't think I'm imposing on you,' she began, 'but as I told you on the telephone, I need to talk to someone and when I went through my list of friends, not one of them seemed the right person. They're either too close to the family or people from the world of medicine who haven't a clue about the world of commerce. You came out as the natural choice, if I can put it that way.' She looked at me appraisingly. 'You're detached from it all and have many contacts. I hope you don't mind being used like that.'

We talked generalities over lunch in the restaurant, enjoying each other's company and then returned to the lounge for coffee.

'Now then,' I said, 'suppose you start telling me all about it. We may have a crowded afternoon ahead of us.'

'Fine,' she replied. 'I'll try and keep the story as precise as I can.'

I sat quietly and listened.

'I have told you that my father was a doctor and he died a little over three years ago. He moved to Lymington as a General Practitioner as a young man, and married my mother, who was a local girl.

We were a normal country-doctor family, lived in a pleasant house, and were part of the local social scene. I went through the usual phases from ponies to pop groups and went to a girls' boarding school in Bournemouth.

'Daddy had a boat and we spent a lot of time sailing. We weren't rich, but we were not poor either. His income was from his group general practice and over the years he moved up to be one of the senior partners. He didn't know much about money matters but saved in the normal way a man in his position does. He had savings in a Building Society, a mortgage on the house, a few minor investments plus life insurance and generally no worries in the world outside his work, which he enjoyed anyway.' She paused.

'One of many similar families throughout the country,' I stated. 'Rather like my own, in fact.'

'Yes', she agreed and then smiled. 'In a moment I'll get to the point but I thought I should give you a bit of background first.'

27

'Don't hurry,' I said, easily. 'You're doing well.'

Pat continued. 'Being a local doctor, my father inevitably got snippets of information about local matters. You can't help it. He heard about some land that was for sale outside a nearby village, about fifteen acres I think it was. I gather he talked it over with his bank manager chum and decided to buy it. It was really agricultural land, bordering on to the village. He'd gone into it with the local planning people and been told that it was unlikely that he would get residential planning permission in the immediate future, but there was always the chance in the long term. He liked the idea of owning land and, as he said, having taken advice, there was little chance that he could lose on it. He didn't like borrowing money, so he cleaned out his various savings of about £20,000 and bought the land.' She paused and sipped her coffee, then continued:

'Two years later the miracle happened. That area on the side of the village was suddenly re-zoned as building land for three new estates of houses and Daddy's land was in a prime position. All sorts of people came clamouring to buy it and he eventually sold most of it to a development company for £300,000. He was advised by his bank manager to keep back a few acres from the development company on the basis that they would pay even more in the future for what was left. They had the option to do this at a price to be agreed when the time came. You can imagine we were rather stunned at our good fortune.' She paused again and I poured her some more coffee. 'Am I boring you?' she asked, suddenly concerned.

'No. Go on, I'm fascinated. There has to be a catch somewhere, I gather.'

'Well, yes and no. Daddy had made a profit of £280,000 on the land he had sold and, of course the tax people wanted their share. When all this was sorted out, he was presented with a tax bill for about £170,000. He should have paid up and been happy with his £110,000 profit but, well, we're all human. You think you've got £280,000 and then suddenly you're asked to hand over a large slab of it to the Inland Revenue and the thought sticks in your gullet. Daddy talked to his accountant and the upshot of it was that he was advised to pay up and be grateful for what he'd have left. This, of course, now in retrospect, is what he should have done. Anyway, before doing this he decided to take further advice — a not unreasonable thought and, I must admit, I too went along with the idea.'

She paused again as she reached for the sugar granules. Placing a generous spoonful in her coffee, she then went on:

'You know how some of the weekend papers are full of financial advertisements from Building Societies and Insurance Companies and also from London Insurance Brokers and Financial Advisors? Advertisements about tax planning, mitigating tax, arranging financial affairs and such like. They all say virtually the same thing, and no doubt there's a need for such people.'

I nodded.

'Well, Daddy decided he'd go and

talk to a company called McNab Brown McNab, with an office in Berkeley Square. He chose this company because he'd read somewhere that they were advising Raymond Flyte on matters concerning his investments and tax matters.'

I interposed. 'I was wondering when he was going to rear his head.'

'Daddy,' she continued, 'not knowing anything about these things, took the simple view that if they were good enough to advise a magnate like Raymond Flyte, they must be a pretty switched-on crowd of people.'

'Yes,' I said. 'I would too.'

'Anyway, he made an appointment and came up to London to see them and talked over his problem. He came back very impressed, saying that they seemed to be very nice people, had lovely offices, had given him lunch in their own dining-room and, what is most important, had outlined a plan whereby he wouldn't have to pay any tax at all. He said he'd got lost about how they proposed to do it after their first ten minutes of explanation, but they told him there was a tax loophole in the present laws, and what they had in mind was quite legal at the time, although they had information that the Inland Revenue were working to close the gap, which would undoubtedly happen before too long. He said there had been no fast talking. It was all very calm and relaxed and, when he explained that the workings of the scheme were beyond him, he was invited to come up again, with his own accountant, to have the various steps spelt out.

'Their fee for saving him £170,000 of tax would be ten per cent of the amount saved, if he decided to go ahead. He was very impressed. He talked to his local accountant and they went up to London together for another meeting. Daddy was soon lost again but his accountant went on probing and questioning and the meeting lasted for about two hours. On the train back home, he asked his accountant what he thought of the whole thing. The man admitted that there were certain aspects that he would like to check but in general principle, the scheme was brilliant and, most importantly, appeared to be quite legal.

'The accountant conferred with a local tax barrister, who was also a qualified accountant himself. He too confirmed that the scheme was brilliant and legal but that the Inland Revenue were well aware of the loophole and it wouldn't be open for long.

'Daddy's accountant therefore agreed when Daddy decided to go along with the tax avoidance plan. They made an appointment to go to London again with a view to proceeding and Daddy came back that same evening, grinning all over his face and saying he hadn't had so much fun for a long time. He told us what happened but I can't really remember the details. Basically, as far as I can make out, they met in a boardroom which had a galaxy of telephones in various positions around the table. The meeting started off with his handing over his personal cheque for £17,000, which it was made quite clear was their non-returnable fee. Company stamps and seals were produced, along with a lot of other legal paraphernalia. Telephone calls were made, all sorts of pieces of paper were signed and then everybody smiled and shook hands — the scheme was now in operation.

'Daddy bought his accountant a few large gins on the train home to celebrate the saving of £170,000 in one day, less the fee of £17,000.'

She stopped and looked at me.

'What an incredible story,' I said amazed. 'I think I've heard vaguely about such things happening but I didn't really believe them.'

'It's all quite true,' Pat confirmed. 'I must have heard my father tell the story a dozen times with his accountant, bank manager and other friends present. Of course, there was more to it than that, but that's the gist of it.'

'So what went wrong?' I asked, now really hooked.

'That's the inevitable question, and there's a very simple answer. The Inland Revenue exerted pressure, as was expected, to close the gap in the law and three years later the government did so.

What wasn't expected though was that Parliament, in changing the law, should make it retrospective — which I gather is a fairly unusual step.'

'What exactly do you mean by that?'

'When the law was passed, it was backdated so that my father and thousands of others would have to pay the tax anyway. I suppose it's quite understandable, since the Treasury was losing tens of millions of pounds because of the loophole.'

'So your father had to pay-up in the end. What did the bright boys at McNab Brown McNab have to say?'

'They didn't really want to know. They said that they had explained that the loophole would almost certainly be closed but that they couldn't forecast that the change in the law would be backdated. They virtually shrugged their shoulders and said it was bad luck.'

'Keeping, of course, your father's £17,000.'

'Of course. Plus a few thousand other similar fees. Daddy's accountant read somewhere that over the three years before the law was changed, it was estimated that they'd taken something like twenty-two million pounds in fees. There were other companies too, of course, who operated the scheme when they learnt about it. So some big money was made in a short space of time.'

'Christ,' I said, 'that is big. Still your father had the balance left over after he'd paid the taxman.'

'That's just the problem. He didn't.'

'Don't tell me there's more?' I asked.

'I'm afraid so,' she replied.

I glanced at my watch and said, 'It's two-thirty now. I haven't told you but I've arranged to go into my office to look at some files on Raymond Flyte. Would you like to come with me? It will take about twenty minutes to get there in a taxi. Will that be long enough for you to finish your story?'

She had been earnest and frowning slightly before, but suddenly her face cleared.

'Of course. I'd love to. Anyway,' she added with a laugh, 'I'm dying to go to the loo.'

'You go then, and I'll settle up here.

I'll see you at the front entrance in a few minutes.'

As we sped through the busy London streets, seated in a taxi, I said: 'Right. We got to that part when you said that your father didn't keep the rest of the money. What happened?'

'I can only tell you what his accountant explained to me. Apparently, as the law had been made retrospective, the tax had been owing for three years or so. It seems that the tax people could charge interest on this if they chose to do so — and they did. Added to that was an extra complication. Daddy had signed some papers agreeing to sell the *extra* bit of land to the same development company. This, and don't ask me how or why, apparently put the tax he owed into a different category — higher tax that is, plus more interest.'

'But he would still have something left, surely?'

'Perhaps normally, but unfortunately he had his heart attack and died. That meant that everything had to be looked at again. There were the inevitable delays associated with such a tangle. It was only recently, three years after he died, that the final bill from the taxman was presented. That makes roughly six years since he entered into the tax-avoidance scheme which didn't work, plus a higher rate of tax because of the extra bit of land, plus six years' compound interest. I don't understand how or why but the accumulated tax bill added up to £317,000 against the estate that he left. This means that there isn't anything at all. Theoretically he actually owes money.'

'Bloody hell,' I said. 'It sounds impossible.'

'I wish it were. Now you can understand why I need help.'

2

In the press cuttings library there were several large envelopes waiting for me. Pat Sheriden and I seated ourselves at one of the tables. I pulled photographs from the largest one and flicked through them. There were photographs taken at race-courses and other sporting events, banquets, social occasions, even royal occasions, weddings, business conferences, directors' meetings and international functions. In all of them one person dominated the scene as the centre of attention. This man was dark with well groomed hair, greying at the temples. He had a well-built stocky figure and was always immaculately dressed for the particular occasion. His strong face was set over a firm chin but in all the pictures the photographer had caught an impish, almost boyish grin, overset by dark, slightly mocking eyes.

'Well, there he is,' I said spreading

the photographs out with a sweep across the table.

'He looks quite different to what I expected,' Pat said. 'Rather a nice-looking man.'

'Yes,' I said, 'a sort of cheeky face. He looks as if he takes care of himself too — physically I mean. I wonder how old he is.'

I turned over several of the photographs and read on the back.

'Here we are. Let's see he must be fifty-three now. This one was taken last year when he was knighted. He doesn't look as old as that.'

'No,' she agreed, 'he hasn't let the good life run him to seed.'

We read through all the detailed captions, then stacked the photographs back in the envelope. The other envelopes held press cuttings and reports of Flyte's various business activities: companies bought, companies sold, commercial arrangements entered into, and so on. There were interviews on matters of financial, trade union, or industrial concern. It would have taken us many hours to read them all in detail. We could do no more than skim over them. Suddenly Pat said:

'Here, look at this.'

She handed me a photograph of a smiling Raymond Flyte, holding a glass in his hand, at the centre of an informal group of men and women. The caption read: *'Raymond Flyte, the entrepreneur, with the directors and guests of financial consultants, McNab Brown McNab in their new offices in Berkeley Square. Mr Flyte disclosed that he is allowing this company to handle a portion of his investment.'* There followed a short commentary on the services offered by the company.

A second cutting was pinned to the photograph with the headline *'McNab Brown McNab'* and underneath the caption *'Flyte Denial'*. The cutting read: *'Following the publicity that has been given to the investigations in hand by the Inland Revenue and the Department of Trade and Industry on a widespread tax-avoidance scheme originated and operated by McNab Brown McNab,*

*Investment and Tax Consultants, Mr
Raymond Flyte stated today that he had
severed all connections with this firm.
When asked his opinion of the scheme,
Mr Flyte replied that he thought the
matter was most unfortunate. He denied
that he was ever personally involved in
the tax-avoidance schemes that McNab
Brown McNab operated. He stated that
his own accountants looked after such
matters for him.'*

'Look at the dates,' said Pat. 'That first
photograph there was taken not all that
long before my father went to see them.
The denial statement was made about the
time that Daddy got his rude awakening
letter from the Inland Revenue.'

'Whatever Flyte's involvement with
McNab Brown McNab,' I said, 'he
wanted to make sure he came out
of it as 'Mr Clean' and it appears
he's done so. There's nothing there in
either statement that actually implicates
him closely with the company. The first
does no more than express a limited
confidence in them. There's a complete
severing of ties and a disclaimer in the

second. Mind you, I know only too well that what people know or suspect is quite different from what gets printed.'

I leaned back in my chair.

'Let's stop for a moment, Pat, and think. What really are we looking for? Your father has been taken for a legal ride by entering into a scheme which he shouldn't have done. On the other hand the scheme might have worked out, in which case you would have been delighted for him. Viewing it coldly and dispassionately, the McNab Brown McNab attitude of 'we regret, but hard luck' is not an unrealistic one, viewed at least from the hard end of the spectrum. That's no consolation to you but it's one that hard-headed business men take.'

'But if a reputable businessman like Raymond Flyte lets it be known that he is associated with something, that's tantamount to endorsing it,' Pat said.

'How do you know that he knew anything about it?' I asked. 'Because he let them make some investments for him it doesn't mean that he was implicated in all their activities. Come on, Pat, be fair.'

She gave me a penetrating look and said, 'So you think I'm wasting my time. Is that it?'

'Not in the least. But let me say, quite understandably, that you're emotionally involved. I am supposed to be an objective, impartial reporter — and I'm looking at it like that for the moment. I'm the first to admit that two small press cuttings don't in any way give us the whole picture, despite all the other coverage here. There is one thing that puzzles me, however. We have a mass of information covering the spread of Flyte's business activities over the past ten years and lots of glossy pictures of his social life. There's nothing here at all though that tells us what he is like as a person now that he has made the big time. There's not one word about his activities before the age of forty-three. What's his background? Where was he born? There's nothing. Does he come from a wealthy family, Eton, Cambridge, a Merchant Bank, that sort of thing? Or did he make it the hard way? There's a *Who's Who* over there — let's look him up.'

There was a brief entry that had not yet been updated to include his recent knighthood. It told us nothing that we did not know already, except for the clubs he belonged to. It listed his interests and hobbies as 'diverse'. We learnt, however, that he was born in Middlehurst, Yorkshire.

Pat stood beside me, looking rather downcast, and I said buoyantly:

'Cheer up. I'm beginning to sense something not quite right in all this,' and I gestured to the table with all the press cuttings spread over it. 'There are many successful men who shun publicity but they are usually the quiet sort. There are others who are born extroverts and hog the limelight and the media on all possible occasions. This man apparently — and I emphasise apparently — suddenly became an extrovert in the past ten years. It can happen that way, I suppose, but I've got a feeling that we're on to something. Let's delve a bit further.'

'How do we do that?' Pat asked, brightening at my sudden enthusiasm.

I didn't answer but crossed over to

the telephone and dialled an internal number. 'Henry, you old sod, Tony Roberts here.'

'My boy,' said the voice. 'I heard you were back — exhausted from the harems. When am I going to see you?'

'Now, if that's all right — plus a friend.'

He paused. 'Give me ten minutes and then I'll be clear for a breather.'

'Who was that?' asked Pat.

'Henry Lust, our City Editor. If anyone can shed a little more light on our illustrious knight, he can.'

I had photocopies of the two McNab Brown McNab cuttings made for me and handed the envelopes back. It was fairly late in the afternoon by the time we made our way to Henry Lust's office. Glancing at my watch, I was surprised to see just how long sifting through the press cuttings had taken. As we entered, he was talking on the telephone.

'Sorry, George,' he said, 'I've got to go. There's a very important event just come in.' He put down the receiver and rose to his feet. He ignored me, went straight to Pat, took her hand and lead her to a chair.

'My dear,' he said, charmingly. 'What's a lovely girl like you doing with a disreputable character like this? Don't you know about this man? We had to smuggle him out of Saudi Arabia for the good of his health. Terrible diseases there are out there and I hear he's contracted all of them. What you need is a nice, quiet, middle-aged, mature man of experience to look after you.'

She caught the merriment in his voice and laughed.

'Need I tell you,' I retorted, 'we say Lust by name and Lust by nature. Not original — but accurate.'

'Not true,' he said in an injured tone. 'Just professional jealousy concerning a more successful colleague.'

'You'll hardly believe it,' I told Pat, 'but this old would-be Casanova has a beautiful wife that he adores, plus three lovely daughters. He runs a mile when any of the girls call his bluff at an office party.'

We all laughed and he pointed at a

chair for me and went round behind his desk.

'Henry,' I began, 'this isn't entirely a social call. I'm looking into something for Pat and wondered whether you could help us.'

His manner changed, he asked: 'Looking into what?'

'I suppose at this stage the answer is Sir Raymond Flyte.'

'Oh, our old friend — Top,' he said easily.

'Who?' I asked.

'Top. Top Flyte. That's the nickname he's acquired. One of the other rags reported on a speech he made to the Institute of Directors. We reported it too, but scaled down. The gist of the speech was that there are various strata in any society, in any country, of any political persuasion. Some people are at the bottom, some in the middle and some at the top. He went on about encouragement for people to progress to the top and being given better rewards when they get there. Usual sort of thing we've all heard before. Anyway, some hack in his column referred to him as 'Top' Flyte, and it's stuck. I understand he quite likes it.'

I handed over the photocopies I had brought with me and he glanced over them. He looked at both of us in turn and then said:

'I think you'd better tell me what this is all about.'

Pat looked at me and nodded. I gave him a condensed version of Pat's father's financial involvement and the aftermath. Henry's expression became more serious as I revealed the repercussions of Dr Sheriden's actions. When I'd finished, he leant back in his capacious chair and whistled.

'Boy, oh boy, what a story. Regrettably I've heard this all before. It amounts to inexperienced people trying to join the rat-race and getting their fingers burnt. Please,' he said, looking at Pat, 'that's no disrespect to your father. It's more an indictment of the system, or one could say of human nature, whichever way you look at it.' His normally cheerful face looked genuinely sad. I caught a despairing glance from Pat.

'Henry,' I said, 'I know those cuttings can't possibly give the whole truth about Raymond Flyte's connection. Was he in fact involved?'

'Of course. Up to his neck in it, or so I've heard. Not in any way that would implicate him though — he's too clever for that.'

'Looking at his photographs he looks a pleasant enough man. Is he?' Pat asked.

'My God,' said Henry, 'what a question. How can any man who's made a million, let alone multimillions, be described as pleasant? And I've met a lot of them. It may sound a strange thing to say, but it's a hard life being a millionaire. For most, first they've got to make it and then they've got to keep it. Neither is easy.'

Pat asked: 'Is there no single characteristic common to all of them?'

Henry thought for a time, frowning and tapped his desk with a pencil.

'In a sense they are a mixed bunch but there's not one, but a number of common characteristics. Firstly, the thing they all have in common is their ego. Whatever they may say themselves, they are dedicated to making money with all that that entails — to satisfy themselves. The second is that their work, is not *work*. They really enjoy what they're doing. Consequently the hours they put in are phenomenal.

'The third thing,' he continued, 'is that they've all got an internal spring inside them which few of us can understand. It's wound up tight in their younger days and drives them on until it runs down. In some it never does run down. However much money they make, however much power and control they obtain, they always want more. It's like a drug.

'The last thing that is common to all, and the characteristic that acquires them enemies, is the ability to be utterly ruthless. They can walk over people on their way up without a backward glance or a twinge of conscience. Add to that a basic feeling of insecurity which a lot of them have, despite their wealth, and they just have to keep on going. Insecurity allied with discontent have driven a lot of men to become millionaires. Sounds odd, doesn't it?'

'Which specific bracket would you put Raymond Flyte into?'

Henry thought for a time and then said:

'As a snap judgement I would say that he is a very clever wheeler-dealer with the charm of a smart confidence trickster. That could apply to many successful men in the City — and elsewhere. I think I would describe him as a hard man with a charming exterior — when he wants to show it. As a matter of fact, I quite like him, compared to many tycoons I've met.'

'The thing that puzzles me though,' I said, 'is that there's very little in the files on his personal life.'

'That's not unusual,' Henry replied, 'and you should know why. We print what people want to read, otherwise we wouldn't sell our newspaper. Deviate from that basic theme and we'll all be out of work. Flyte's star started shining about nine or ten years ago and has gone on getting brighter. His lifestyle is not dissimilar to many others like him. He collected a young bride a few years ago — she'd been a top model from an aristocratic family, as I recall it. I've met her — very attractive. But none of that's really big news.'

'I understand. But what did he do on the way up? Where did he come from?' I asked, trying to gather as many facts as possible.

'I believe he started up North with nothing very much. There's nothing very unusual about making it from humble beginnings. Perhaps he likes to keep quiet about his origins — so do lots of people.' He paused and said, 'I know you, Tony, you're up to something, aren't you?'

'Truthfully, Henry, I don't know at the moment. It's just a gut feeling I have and I'd like to follow my nose. But please keep quiet about it.'

'Understood,' he said, looking hard at me. 'I know that runny nose of yours. If it gets you anywhere, you'll let me know, won't you?'

He looked at his watch, leapt to his feet and came round to Pat, his mood changing immediately. She got up.

'I can't thank you enough for all this background information you've given us,' she said holding out her hand.

Henry smiled and taking her hand gave it a gentle kiss.

'Not at all, my dear. I only hope I've been of some assistance.'

As we walked towards the door, he seemed to have a thought. 'If you like, meet me in the Crown and Thistle at six o'clock, I might just have something more for you. Grab a corner table.'

I felt a sudden sense of excitement until he added: 'If I'm not there by seven, don't wait any longer but call me tomorrow.'

★ ★ ★

We were in the pub soon after opening time at five-thirty, which was just as well. By six o'clock it was comfortably full of people having a drink before journeying home. I was getting a little anxious as six-thirty approached, when Henry came through the door. Behind him was a small, slightly-built, middle-aged man in a shabby grey suit. A bald head accentuated his long pallid face and sad brown eyes. He followed Henry through the throng of drinkers over to our table in the corner.

Henry introduced him. 'This horrible looking creature, whom I've brought to talk to you, goes by the distinguished name of Fred.' He turned to Fred, smiling, 'These are the friends that I told you about. Why don't you go and get us a drink while I find another chair.' He thrust a five pound note in Fred's hand as he turned towards the bar.

Quite some minutes later we were all seated at the table, drinks topped up when Henry continued in the same vein. 'This somewhat dog-eared specimen of humanity is not entirely what he might appear. Under that bald dome of his is a brain that's like a sponge. In some areas that brain's not too bright, but in others it collects, collates and stores information. You press a button and out come answers to questions about what's going on in the square mile around us.

The button you have to press tonight is a few drinks and a fiver. That's right isn't it, Fred?'

'Absolutely, Mr Lust,' Fred said in a surprisingly educated voice. He looked down, turning his glass around and around.

'Fred here used to be a successful managing clerk in a firm of solicitors, until he became a naughty boy. He was locked away as one of Her Majesty's guests. He liked it so much that when they let him out he committed the same crime again and he went back for another rest, at the taxpayers' expense. Isn't that right, Fred?'

'Yes, Mr Lust,' he replied shyly. 'But must you talk about it like that?'

'Why not?' said Henry. 'Everyone who should know, does know — and I want to warn this lovely lady here. What did you go to prison for, Fred?'

Fred squirmed in his seat and looked embarrassed. He glanced at Pat and then down again at the table.

'Bigamy,' he whispered.

'That's right,' Henry agreed. 'Would

you believe it? Not content with one wife, he goes and marries two more. Doesn't do things by halves, our Fred. So they locked him up. They let him out to be greeted by three weeping women at the gates and off he runs to Birmingham, where, blow me, if he doesn't collect another wife. So he's locked up again. Now he spends his time dodging all four of them, don't you, Fred?'

'Well, it's all a bit difficult,' the little man replied quietly.

Henry laughed and gave Fred a hearty slap on the back as a gesture of no hard feelings and Fred responded with a sheepish smile.

'Well,' Henry began, 'Fred here has things to tell you.' He downed the remainder of his pint. 'I'm off now.'

As he rose from the table, he whispered to me: 'Don't forget, no more than three drinks and a fiver. Any more and he'll go all amorous again and collect yet another wife. We don't want him locked up — we need him.' He patted Fred on the shoulder. 'You can rely on what Fred tells you — he only deals in gilt-edged.'

When Henry had gone, Fred got more drinks and on his return drew his chair close up to the table.

'I gather you wanted to know about 'Top' Flyte and McNab Brown McNab,' he stated confidentially.

I pulled the photocopies of the two press cuttings out of my pocket and handed them to him. He glanced at them and smiled weakly.

'Let me tell you what I've heard,' he volunteered. 'It seems that Flyte met a very bright young accountant called William Jackson, who outlined to him a scheme whereby people who were faced with large capital gains tax bills could avoid paying them — all quite legal and above board because of a loophole in the tax law. Flyte had the scheme checked and double-checked by his own firm of accountants, a firm, incidentally, that he owns. Tax barristers were consulted and retired senior Inland Revenue people, who had now become tax advisors to commerce, looked at it. It all checked out as being valid, legal and very astute. The Revenue boys weren't going to like it — the people who operated the scheme weren't going to get any medals for popularity but until the gap in the law was closed, some big money was going to be made. This, of course, is exactly what Flyte wanted to hear. It was really a question then of how he could take advantage of the scheme while, at the same time, keeping himself detached from it.'

Fred paused and took a deep drink at the pint of beer in front of him.

'There are a lot of aspiring money-makers in the City, looking for a chance. Flyte chose two such bright young insurance brokers with lots of charm and the right look about them. He wanted them to front a respectable business that would be the cover for the tax-avoidance scheme. He suggested that they go it alone and set up their own company. They would be joint Managing Directors, and would take in William Jackson as a co-director to advise on tax matters. It would be a prestigious set up and, although he would not personally be part of it, he would guarantee their bank account.

'He told them that he was motivated by wishing to help aspiring young men and apparently said, almost as a throwaway line, that he knew it took time to build up a successful business, so he wouldn't charge them interest on any money he put into their account, on condition that, when things improved, he would receive two-thirds of the gross profits. Since Flyte wanted everything done on a grand scale, and the young men were able to pay themselves substantial salaries as joint Managing Directors, they readily agreed to the terms. It didn't seem unreasonable to them — in fact, they were delighted to accept the opportunity. The two bright sparks got cracking, found lovely offices in Berkeley Square, pressed on with the recruitment of suitable retired Service officers, attractive secretaries, had a press launch backed up by national PR and advertising — and were in business.'

'Just a moment,' I said. 'Why retired Service officers? What do they know about insurance, tax schemes and investments?'

Fred took another pull on his pint and said, 'That's just the point. Flyte advised his two hopefuls that there was a vast untapped reservoir of good, educated and intelligent men who had been forced to retire early and who would welcome a new career in something they would see as prestigious.'

He took another drink. 'It's like this, you see. Amongst other things, our Raymond is a bit of a psychologist — he wouldn't be where he is if he wasn't. Ask an ex-Service officer to become a salesman and he'll look down his nose. Ask him to become an 'Investment Consultant', tell him you'll train him, give him a reasonable salary plus commission, a desk at a good address with colleagues of the same type and background — and he suddenly becomes very interested. He doesn't realise that most people in the nasty big commercial world where he hasn't been before are selling something to somebody. He's really only becoming a salesman but with a fancy handle attached that he can boast about in his golf club. Service officers also have advantages because they're usually good mixers and have a certain presence about them. Plus something which they started off with and which has been developed — honesty. So they're given three weeks' training, told to call themselves 'Mister' and launched onto the unsuspecting public.'

'Three weeks,' exclaimed Pat. 'What can they learn in three weeks?'

'Only the very basic terminologies — but they learn more as they go along. After all, they are intelligent men who really believe they're starting out in a new career.'

'And they go out and advise people about their money?' asked Pat again.

'Yes and no,' Fred replied. 'Mr Smith, say, sees one of the nicely worded advertisements in a Sunday newspaper and he wants some advice about what to do with his money. He believes that the big boys in London, who are close to the centre of things, can advise him. So he writes a letter, phones up, or fills in the coupon in the paper. A pleasant educated man talks to him on the telephone, suggests an exploratory discussion and one of the retired officers turns up at his home by appointment. His visitor is a professional looking type, doesn't try to sell him anything and is able to complete a detailed questionnaire about Mr Smith's financial position. He goes off promising to send Mr Smith a recommendation plan. Our investment consultant returns to his office and discusses Mr Smith with his bosses, who outline their recommendations. From standard pro forma letters and layouts, one of the dolly-birds types the whole thing up and off it goes. A week later Mr Smith receives a personalised folder through the post.

'In it is a report, beautifully typed on heavy cream notepaper, giving him the impression that a panel of experts have spent days analysing his financial future and, of course, he's suitably impressed. Ignoring his bank manager and his friendly local broker, he locks himself into total strangers in London.

'He may, of course, be prudent and visit them. What does he find? Expensive, prestigious offices, good manners and a cup of coffee or tea in a quiet visitors' discussion room.

'No hard-sell, just quietly confident professional people close to the hub of the money centre of the world. Don't get me wrong. Most firms who do this kind of thing are decent, honest and reliable, but there are a few that could be called 'sharp'. Raymond Flyte knew all about these things when he funded the new firm.'

'What about the name McNab Brown McNab?' asked Pat. 'Who were they?'

'Nobody. They didn't exist. You don't have to use your actual names. You just think of a name that sounds suitable for a particular company, check that someone else hasn't got it, and then register the name at Company House.'

He drained his pint. I gave him some more money and he went off to replenish our glasses.

Once on our own Pat turned to me and said, 'I'm beginning to feel a bit sick — not literally — just mentally. I'm not used to this kind of thing. I haven't led a sheltered life by any means but — well — things go on that you don't even think about.'

'I suppose I've seen a lot more of this kind of thing being a newspaperman. I think I told you something about my disenchantment with what I saw in the Middle East.'

'Yes,' she said, 'but listening to Henry today, who's a very nice man, and now little Fred, well, they just seem to take it as being — normal.'

Fred returned with the drinks, placed them carefully on the table and sat down. He took a large gulp from his fresh pint before saying, 'You can probably guess the rest. William Jackson's brilliant scheme took off like a rocket and vast profits were made in only three years. It's said that Top Flyte took fifteen million as his share and the three directors took the rest. When all the fuss started, the firm closed down.' He picked up his glass again.

'You mean they no longer exist?' Pat asked with undisguised amazement.

'That's right. Went into voluntary

liquidation. The staff were given one month's salary and goodbye. The doors were closed and that was it. Everything was paid up, no debts or nasty aftermath. Flyte made sure of that. Just a lot of sad and sorry clients who wished they'd never heard of McNab Brown McNab.'

'And Flyte made fifteen million pounds?' I said.

'Well, not precisely. He made sure the money went through his accountants' books and there was a heavy wack of tax to pay. But he came out of it very nicely, even then. He doesn't fiddle around himself — makes sure that all's square with the taxman. Can't afford to get caught.'

He drank more of his pint rather enjoying his role of information-giver. 'Anything else on 'Top' I can help you with?' he asked with new-found confidence.

'No,' I said, 'I think you've told us enough. If I think of anything else, I'll contact Mr Lust.'

'Well, if I can help, he'll know how to find me.' He drained his pint and looked at his glass. 'You couldn't — could you?' he asked.

I gave him a pound for another pint and a five pound note that he looked at sadly. Pat took her wallet out of her handbag and gave him another fiver. He picked up the money and his glass, stood up, and said, 'Thank you, miss, and you, sir.'

He turned and walked away. We watched him deposit his glass on the bar and go out of the door.

Suddenly I laughed. 'Why did you do that?' I asked. 'You heard what Henry said.'

'I just felt sorry for the poor pathetic little man.'

'Pathetic little man! He enjoyed every minute of it,' I grinned.

She smiled. 'Perhaps you're right.'

I looked at my watch and asked: 'What about dinner?'

She shook her head. 'Thanks, but I really must get back home. Thank you for all you've done. I'm sorry to have imposed on you like this.'

'Imposed? Nonsense. Like our Fred,

I've enjoyed every minute of it. The thing is, what happens now? Our man Flyte is certainly no knight in shining armour, but I wonder how many of them are.'

'Do you think I'll find a taxi to take me to Waterloo Station?' Pat asked as she got up. 'I don't feel like the underground.'

'I'll come with you,' I volunteered, 'I'm going to stay up here tonight anyway.'

In the taxi, I said, 'I have an idea forming about things. When I've thought it out, perhaps I could phone you.'

'Yes,' she replied. 'I'll be in most evenings. I'd love you to.'

Walking across Waterloo Station she slipped her arm through mine as we headed towards her platform. At the barrier she turned to me and said: 'There's only a few minutes — don't come any further.' Leaning forward she planted a gentle kiss on my lips, then quickly turned and headed for the train.

3

In the morning I caught an early train home and was there by lunchtime. My father was relaxing watching the one o'clock news on TV before my mother called us for lunch. I waited until the meal was over and we were drinking coffee before I broached my father with the subject on my mind.

'There's something you might be able to help me with,' I began to gain his attention.

'What's that then,' he replied with a grin. 'I know it can't be money. You've got a tidy amount tucked away.'

'No. It's not that. It's something I'm trying to do for a friend of mine. Have you got any strong reliable contacts up North, in Middlehurst? Someone who has been there a long time?'

'We've three branches up there of varying sizes. I know the senior manager of one reasonably well. But how far do you want to go back?'

'Possibly fifty years,' I replied. 'I want to find out about a man who was born and I think grew up there.'

'Good heavens,' my father laughed, 'almost nobody goes back that far. Certainly not the manager that I know. This is not banking business, I imagine.' He eyed me a shade suspiciously. 'I thought you newspaper people had your own sources of information in every town and city in the country.'

'We have, but this is something where I don't want to use the usual sources. It's something I want to keep to myself — for the time being anyway.'

He finished his coffee, looking thoughtful. 'Come to think of it,' he said suddenly, 'there is someone . . . I've met him a number of times on Rotary Club conventions. He's a solicitor in Middlehurst, who joined his firm there as a young man. He certainly goes back fifty years. Perhaps he would be your man.'

'Do you think you could phone him for me and ask him if I might contact him?' I asked.

'Can you tell me what it's about?' my father asked growing more intrigued.

'Would you mind if you left that to me? At this stage, it's a bit delicate.'

'Fair enough. I'll do it as soon as I get back to the office.'

He phoned me about an hour later and gave me the name of Mr George Davidson, whom he said was at home today and awaiting my call. He also gave me the number and the name of his firm. My conversation with Mr Davidson was a brief one. I told him it was a confidential matter concerning Sir Raymond Flyte, and I was delighted when he said, 'That young rascal,' and laughed. 'Known him since he was a lad. We used to look after things for him, in a manner of speaking. Big man now though, down in London.'

'Would you mind if I, and possibly a friend of mine, came to talk to you about him?' I asked.

'Well that depends on what you want to talk about,' he replied.

'Just about his general background and how he grew up.' I told a journalistic

71

white lie. 'I'm thinking of researching a book on prominent millionaires and how they made it to the top. I thought he might be a suitable one to include as he's a colourful character.'

'Come and ask your questions if you like,' he replied. 'Whether I answer them depends on what they are. You're right though, he's certainly colourful.' He chuckled again.

I arranged to meet him at his office in two days' time.

That evening I phoned Pat and told her what I had in mind asking her if she'd like to come with me.

'Yes. I would very much,' she said enthusiastically. 'But I'll have to clear things with the Saudi Embassy to get some more leave, but the man I deal with there is very sympathetic. I'll speak to him tomorrow, but I don't think there'll be any problem.'

We arranged to meet at the Grosvenor House Hotel in London the following evening and to travel up to Middlehurst the next day.

★ ★ ★

We had lunch on the fast Inter-City train and arrived in Middlehurst with plenty of time to spare for our afternoon appointment. At the station entrance we decided not to take a taxi to the hotel I had booked, but walked with our small suitcases into the town centre. I had visited the town before and I lead Pat across the damp black-cobbled streets between rows of flat-fronted red-brick Victorian houses, some with their paintwork peeling and others painted in bright garish colours as if to attempt to lift the air of gloom. The marketplace was full of stalls selling cheap goods and, with the sky overcast, the illuminated shop windows cast some warm light onto what was a depressing scene.

'I can understand why Raymond Flyte or anyone else would want to get away from here,' said Pat, looking around her.

'What you're seeing is a typical northern industrial town on a bad day,' I said. 'It started off as a railway town in the last century. Then the textile mills grew up. Since then there have been all sorts of ups and downs as the place has evolved. There's a lot worse than this I can assure you and at least there's beautiful countryside nearby. You want to see this place on a wet windy day in the middle of winter.'

'No thanks,' said Pat, 'this is enough for me.'

We booked into our hotel and then made our way to the offices of Mr Davidson.

He was a large convivial man with a full head of flowing hair that occasionally tumbled into his eyes. He had a strong rosy complexion resembling that of a country farmer, and he looked at us over gold-rimmed half-moon spectacles which seemed to make his countenance even more genial. We talked of my family and how glad he was to meet my father from time to time.

'Now,' he said, the pleasantries at an end. 'Tell me what I can do for you.'

'As I told you on the telephone,' I replied, 'I'm thinking of researching a book on millionaires. I've got some leave on my hands and I thought I'd make a start. I want to try and get some information on the early life of Sir Raymond Flyte.'

He looked at me over the top of his glasses and then, although they were already gleaming, took them off and polished them meticulously with a large red silk handkerchief. He carefully replaced them back on his nose and returned his handkerchief to his pocket.

'Come on, lad,' he said, 'you'll have to do better than that. I've been behind this desk for a very long time now and I usually know when someone isn't telling me the whole truth. I've got a feeling for it. I don't usually talk to newspaper people except as clients, but in your case I was curious because of your father. Now let's have it fair and square or I'll bid you and the young lady good day and wish you a safe journey home.'

He took off his glasses again, examined them for a moment and then put them back on his nose. Pat and I glanced at each other.

'The first thing,' I said, 'is to apologise.'

He put both his hands in the air towards us.

'No need for that,' he insisted. 'It's just my way of getting things straight from the start. You're not the first person I've said that to by a long chalk,' he added, with one of his chuckles. 'Now tell me what you're really up to and if I can help you, I will.'

I told him about Pat, her father and the recent death of her mother. I gave him a summary of the financial tangle her father had got into and how our preliminary researches had led us to him, at this point. All the time he listened quietly, occasionally nodding or asking a brief, relevant question.

'Very, very interesting,' he said. 'Very interesting indeed. I had no idea that young Flyte was the brain behind that scheme. A number of my clients, some of them my oldest friends, have caught a cold because of him. If it is him,' he added hurriedly. 'Although I don't doubt that what you've told me is true. Let me tell you what I can about Raymond

Flyte, without abusing any confidence or privilege. What you'll hear is common knowledge around the town, but it would take you time to ferret it all out.'

A secretary came in with a tray of tea, which she placed on Mr Davidson's desk, indicating that we should help ourselves.

'Young Raymond was born in Crimea Street, which is still there if you want to go and look at it. I don't know the number but it doesn't matter anyway. The houses are all the same — two-up and two-down, with an alley running down the back of them. His father was a maintenance man of some kind in the railway yard. I never knew him but I remember that he was called up in the Second World War and was killed in France. Raymond was only a young lad then, but his mother, and many other girls, found plenty of American troops around to give them a good time. So the usual thing happened and she found herself having a child by her GI boyfriend. When the baby was born, there were complications and she and the child died in childbirth.'

He picked up his teacup took a few sips, a reflective expression in his eyes. After a few moments he continued, 'Raymond was left an orphan with no known relatives, but some friends who lived in the same street took him in to live with them. The Parkinsons, they were, who had a son, Frank, of about the same age. Raymond and Frank went into the textile mill when they left school and, from what I gathered, did well there. They started their own firm and the business went well, but eventually there was a parting of the ways between Raymond and Frank.'

He finished his cup of tea, removed his glasses and polished them again.

'What happened after that you'll have to find out for yourselves,' he went on. 'Raymond Flyte was a client of mine for a time, so what I know about his business affairs is confidential. What I've told you, is nothing more than anyone of my age in the town could have told you. Middlehurst isn't so big that folk don't know one another, and there's not much to do in the evenings except gossip.

'I cannot, however, divulge details of what happened between Raymond and Frank. You'll have to enquire elsewhere.'

'Does this Frank Parkinson still live in Crimea Street?' I asked.

'I'm ahead of you there, lad,' he replied, scribbling on a notepad. 'Here's his address — it's a block of flats. I'm not sure of the number but anyone there will tell you. I should take a bottle of Scotch with you — when you get there, you'll see why.'

He got up from his chair and walked around in front of us.

'I'm glad it's you who has come to ask me these questions. I would not have liked talking to just anybody. People up here, you know, have the reputation of being hard but honest men of business. When they strike a bargain and shake hands on it, it's as good as any written contract, but Flyte wasn't one of our sort, as I suspect you'll find out.'

He escorted us down the stairs to the office entrance, and stood there smiling genially as we went out into the street.

We picked our way along the cobbles of Crimea Street, passing the identical front doors and lace-curtained windows set in the long red-bricked terrace of houses. I bought a bottle of whisky which I carried in a plastic bag and asked in the shop the way to the address we had been given.

We found a number of grey blocks of flats, set around a concrete courtyard on which children were playing. My questions were answered with suspicion but we eventually rode up in a dirty, urine-smelling lift to the fourth floor of one of the blocks, then along a corridor adorned with graffiti, to the flat where we hoped to find Frank Parkinson. Pat stood back as I knocked on the door. After nearly a minute I knocked again and looked at Pat enquiringly. She shrugged her shoulders and signalled for me to try yet again. As I did so, a head appeared out of a door along the corridor, looked at us, and then withdrew. I heard shuffling from inside the flat and a man's voice calling:

'Who is it? Who's there?'

'Is that Mr Parkinson?' I asked.

'Who wants to know?' came the reply.

'My name's Tony Roberts. I have something for you and I want to talk to you.'

'What about?'

'I can only tell you if you'll open the door. It's all right, I'm not selling anything.' As an afterthought I added. 'I'm not after money either. In fact I want to give you something.'

Heads appeared around adjacent doorways, and children came out and stared at us. A lock turned and the door in front of us opened slightly and a grey-haired unshaven face peered out. Before he could say anything, I lifted the whisky bottle and showed it to him.

'Mr Parkinson,' I said, 'I've brought this for you and just want to talk.'

The door opened further.

'Is she with you?' he asked, nodding at Pat.

'Yes. May we come in, please?'

I handed the bottle and the plastic bag to him and we slipped through quickly as the door opened wide, and then closed behind us. We followed him down a short passageway and into a sitting-room. It was untidy and the furniture was well worn, but it was a comfortable room that needed a good clean. What was surprising was that the walls were covered almost from floor to ceiling in pictures. Some were unframed oil paintings on canvas, others were framed watercolours and pastels. I saw the amazement on Pat's face, and the expression on that of Frank Parkinson's as he looked at her. He addressed himself to Pat.

'I don't know why you've come, but the sight of you and a bottle of whisky would open any door,' he said.

'You did all these?' asked Pat.

'Aye. And a lot more besides. Brighten up the place, don't they?'

'They certainly do,' Pat answered. 'May I have a look?'

'Help yourself,' he replied, turning to me. 'I reckon you sound like a bloke from London. Wouldn't have opened the door if I knew you were from these parts. Too many yobbos about these days.'

As he spoke, I got the strong smell of stale alcohol from his breath and noted the bloodshot eyes and the purpled nose of the heavy drinker. I could see that he had once been a good-looking man, but now his features were coarsened, and his body, in soiled shirt and blue jeans, had run to fat. His hands shook as he poured large measures of whisky into doubtfully clean glasses. He smiled when Pat and I asked for water in ours and he carried the glasses to the kitchen tap.

'Yon's a nice-looking lass,' he said to me, as we seated ourselves with difficulty, moving pictures and newspapers onto a plastic table in the corner.

'I'll paint her for you if you'll give me the time. Do it for twenty pounds.'

'Thank you, but we're not here long. I'll give you twenty-five pounds though, if you can tell me something I want to know.'

'And what would that be then?' he asked.

'About Raymond Flyte,' I said.

'That bugger,' he said. 'What do you want to know about him for?'

I told him my white lie about writing a book on millionaires. Without telling him the source, I outlined what we'd learnt from the local solicitor. Then I added:

'What I want to know is what went wrong between the two of you. Plus anything else you can tell us about him.'

He laughed ironically. 'I could write a book about him myself, but they'd be too afraid to publish it. He's a right bastard, he is.'

He filled his glass again with neat whisky.

'This must be worth something to you,' he said. 'And by the look of you both, you're not short of a bob or two. Make it fifty pounds and I'll talk to you until this bottle's empty.'

'All right,' I said. 'Here's twenty-five pounds now and the other half when you've told me all you know.'

He put the money on the ring-marked table under the bottle, by his right hand, lit a cigarette and started to talk. He had a clear voice with a north-country intonation. He kept topping his glass up and almost chainsmoked from the packet of cigarettes on the arm of his chair.

'The first thing you've got to understand,' he said, is that Ray's dad — we called him Ray — and my dad were pals. They worked together, drank together, went to football together and were in and out of each other's houses all the time. My mum and his mum got on well together and Ray and me were in the same class at school. Then the war came, and Ray's dad was called up for the army and mine had to stay at home and carry on working on the railway. You can imagine how it shook my dad when his pal was killed. Ray's mum and my mum both worked in the local factory until Ray's mum took up with her Yank and became pregnant. My dad was furious, especially when this Yank disappeared as soon as he learnt there was a child on the way. Ray used to stay with us a lot in those days, so when his mum died it seemed a natural thing for him to move in with us permanently. The war was over by then and there were quite a few parentless children about who had lost a father at the front or a mother in the bombing. Ray wasn't adopted but with things as they were, the authorities were glad to have one less child to worry about. My dad got seventeen pounds, two shillings and ninepence for all the belongings we sold from Ray's house. I remember the exact figure. Ray told my dad to keep it but he wouldn't have that — so he opened a Post Office account in Ray's name.

'I remember lots of times coming up to our bedroom and finding Ray sitting on the bed, working out how much more interest his money had earned since he'd last looked at it. He was good at arithmetic at school — I was hopeless. Drawing was about the only thing I was any good at. Ray was just like any other kid until he got that Post Office book and then he seemed to change. He took up a newspaper round, mornings and evenings, and on Saturday afternoon, when we went to the football, he was sweeping up in the market or running errands. That savings book became a fixation. I used to ask him why he was doing it and I always got the same answer — 'he liked to see the money grow'.'

Frank filled his tumbler again and lit another cigarette.

'We left school and went into the textile mill that had switched to making carpets after the war.

'At first we were just general dogbodies around the place. Then they found that I liked drawing, so I was allocated to the design office. Ray went on working in every department he could get himself into, and put in as much overtime as he could get. I thought then that it was just for the sake of his precious book, but he really put himself out to learn about everything that was going on, and they thought a lot of him. They made him a supervisor before he was twenty and he was controlling much older men, sorting out problems — and doing it well, too.

'My sister Beryl and Ray started going out together, not that he ever spent any money on her. Just long walks in the country on Sundays — that sort of thing. They became inseparable and people started gossiping.

'My mate and my sister going out together was great news to me, until

Mum found out Beryl was expecting Ray's child. She was nineteen and Ray was just twenty-one. At least he did the right thing and married her, much to everyone's relief. He rented a small flat for them and they moved into it. I remember him showing me his account book at the time. He had two thousand, four hundred pounds in it. In those days it seemed a fortune, and he'd saved it all himself.'

He filled his glass to the top and took a generous slurp. He seemed to have become more relaxed and talkative — presumably the alcohol was now having an effect.

'Shortly after they were married,' he went on, 'he told me that he wanted to go into business on his own. He said he'd found a gap in the market. There was an unfilled demand for high-quality rugs of good design. He knew how to make them, but he wanted a partner who could design them — and that was where I came in. He rented two small lots of premises. In one, I did the designing and Beryl packed and despatched the finished goods. In the other, he manufactured and generally managed things. He explained that one day he'd have the business all under one roof in a modern factory, but in the meantime, we'd have to make do with what we'd got.

'So we pitched in, worked all hours God sent, and took out only very small weekly wages to cover the absolute necessities of life. We took on extra staff of course, in time, as we expanded, but we worked like that for nearly nine years. Ray's ideas and my designs really took off. Ray Flyte Rugs as they were called, was a big success.'

The whisky bottle was no longer very full. Frank put his glass down on the table and sat back.

'One day,' he began slowly, 'Ray phoned through to my office and asked me to come over right away. In his office he had the man who did our books and someone I'd never seen before. On a side table was a pile of our rugs. Ray had some papers in his hand. He brought over one of the rugs and turned it over so that I could see the label on the back. I realised immediately that the label design was of a type we'd had made, but decided not to use — Ray wanted his name on our product.

'It would take too long to tell you all the details of what happened over the next hour. But, in a nutshell, I was accused of having a lucrative sideline by selling our rugs under a different label, through a man who supplied market traders and small retail outlets. Of course I denied it, because it wasn't true, but then in came a man who said he'd swear in court that I'd been the source of his supply and that he could produce numerous other witnesses. I couldn't believe it was happening. Finally, Ray introduced me to his solicitor. This was the man I hadn't recognised when I'd walked in. I can remember Ray standing there and saying, 'Be careful, Frank, I'm advised that you could be charged with the offence of the unauthorised sale of company property for your own personal profit. In the circumstances, I'm not going to call the police and have you charged. You are, however, dismissed immediately from my employ.' I just couldn't believe what was happening.'

'But why?' asked Pat devastated. 'How could he do such a thing to you? What was his purpose?'

'I didn't know until a month later when it was announced in the local press that he'd sold the business for several hundred thousand pounds, along with my very successful design techniques.'

'But you had an interest in the business, didn't you?' I asked.

'I consulted a solicitor. In effect he told me that the agreement I had wasn't worth the paper it was written on. I'd never understood officialdom, and it seems that Ray had formed all sorts of other companies which I didn't even know about. The agreement between us had been drawn up by him and I didn't read it carefully. I just trusted him; he was my mate and married to my sister. It turned out that I was really no more than an employee entitled to a percentage in certain circumstances, and all my designs belonged to Ray.'

'But you were never prosecuted,' Pat

said. 'It was merely some false witnesses against you. Why didn't you fight him?'

'I nearly did,' he replied. 'I went to see my sister Beryl. That was the crunch. She told me that if it ever went to court, she would have to say that she had been worried about stock disappearing that she couldn't account for. Also that there were some false entries in the stockbook in my handwriting. I had helped her out once or twice when she was very busy, but at her dictation. Even my bloody sister was in it,' he said, slurring his words, overcome with both emotion and drink. 'That finished me. I just gave up after that. Can't fight those sort of bastards.'

He closed his eyes and for a moment I thought he was asleep. Pat and I looked at one another and got to our feet. Suddenly he said:

'I reckon I've earned the other twenty-five quid, don't you?'

I put it on the arm of his chair and we walked towards the door.

'Don't forget,' he said suddenly, opening his eyes and looking at Pat, 'if you want your portrait painted, you know where to come.'

He turned and looked at me.

'Good luck with your book. You can include everything I've told you. People should know. Don't tell her you've seen me or she won't talk to you but look up Mrs B J Flyte in the phone book. Churchwood Road, Chilwold. It's near here. My bloody sister. They divorced years ago but she's never remarried. Maybe you'll find out why.'

He turned in his chair and closed his eyes.

We let ourselves out.

★ ★ ★

I talked to the hotel receptionist the following morning and learnt that Chilwold was a residential area just on the outskirts of the town. I met Pat in the dining-room for breakfast and outlined to her how I thought Mrs Beryl Flyte might best be approached. From my room, Pat put a phone call through to her, posing as the personal assistant of Mr Anthony Roberts, the writer. She explained that we were in the area briefly and that it would be very much appreciated if we could have a talk with her about her ex-husband, for a future book. Pat mentioned the woman's viewpoint, suggesting that Mrs Flyte had, no doubt, helped her husband in his earlier career. She was very convincing and I heard her making an appointment for us for eleven o'clock that morning. She put the receiver down with an explosion of breath.

'Well done. How did she sound?' I asked.

'Cautious at first, but it was the bit of flattery that I think did the trick. She sounded rather the 'refined cut-glass' type — if you know what I mean. You were right in having me talk to her. She sounds the sort who'd be impressed by someone having a personal assistant.' Pat looked at me ruefully. 'God,' she said, 'you're turning me into a regular little liar. Just like a reporter — anything for an interview.'

We went by taxi to Chilwold. As we reached the edge of the town, we were in an area of mock-Tudor houses, neat driveways, perfectly kept half-acre gardens and fresh tree-lined roads. An expensive semi-country suburb.

A well-dressed middle-aged woman came to the door and greeted us. Her hair was a pronounced artificial blonde colour. Her face was heavily made-up and she was a little too plump to be fashionable. Despite this, she had a reasonably well-groomed appearance. She lead us through the hall into the lounge at the back of the house, looking on to smooth lawn. The room was well furnished with pseudo-antique oak furniture and a heavy, excessively large, three-piece suite. Everything was obviously expensive but the house lacked a homely feel and good taste. Mrs Flyte invited us to sit down in the two deep armchairs, while she brought a tray of coffee through from the kitchen.

'I'm intrigued to know how you knew I lived here,' she said.

'Miss Sheriden is my right hand,' I replied. 'It was very easy for her to track you down. Your former husband is a very well-known man you know.'

'You've met him, of course.' It was a statement.

'No I haven't. When I'm researching I like to talk to as many people as possible before I meet my subject. It helps me form some sort of perspective on him — or her.' I took the cup of coffee being offered.

'And this book is about Raymond, my ex-husband?' she asked.

'No. Not entirely.' I was becoming a practiced liar myself. 'He's one of a group of business tycoons that I want to write about. I'm sure, like other wives I've talked to, you must have been a big support to him in his early days.' I made a pretence of consulting my notebook. 'I believe that you married quite young.'

'Yes. Sir Raymond grew up here in Middlehurst. We married when he started up his first business.' She was obviously pleased to have been married to a man who had been knighted.

'How did you meet?' asked Pat.

'He was on the management side of the Verity Carpet Company and I was there too. Just for something to do really — in an administrative capacity, of course.' She said it in away that inferred that she was not the sort of person who would have had anything to do with people from the shop-floor.

'Did you help your husband when he branched out on his own?'

'Oh, yes. He had money of his own and didn't like the idea of working for someone else for the rest of his life.

'He was always very ambitious and hardworking. Oh yes, I helped him considerably in those early days. I worked with him — in the office. It helped to keep the overheads down and keep the money in the family.' She laughed nervously.

'What kind of a business was it?' I asked.

'Don't you know? Of course, why should you? We made household rugs. You know the type. Thick rectangle, oval or round rugs with beautiful designs. Anyone with the know-how can make rugs — the designs on them have to be special, though. Raymond always had a flair for spotting a gap in the market, as he used to call it. That and detecting future trends. That's why he sold the business to Verity Carpets, the firm where he started.'

'Why was that?' I asked.

'I suppose I'll have to explain.' She laughed, rather patronisingly. 'You are too young to remember that far back. During the war, manufacture of the traditional Axminster and Wilton carpets had stopped completely. It was only after the war that it got going again. People in those days used to buy carpet squares or runners of whatever quality they could afford for their homes. They put rugs down on the bare parts of the floor areas wherever they felt they were needed. Only the very wealthy were able to afford wall-to-wall fitted carpets that most people are so used to now. This is why our rug business did so well at that time. Then carpets manufactured by what was called the tufting process arrived and were very much cheaper. In the early days people called them 'those cheap rubber-backed things', but my Raymond saw a whole new form of manufacture was opening up which would revolutionise the carpet industry. 'Fitted carpets for the masses', he called it — and he was right again.

'Anyway, he saw what was coming and forecast that there would always be a market for rugs, particularly on the export side, but it wasn't going to grow as it had done before. So he sold out to Verity Carpets here, and joined their board of directors. But he now owns the company, you know.' She picked up her bone-china cup and began to sip from it.

'No, I didn't. When did that happen?'

'Not until much later, when he really got big,' she replied.

'And the rug company you started. What happened to that?'

'That's still going, only in different, modern premises now — all part of the same plant. The products haven't changed much, though. We brought out some very good designs and many of the original ones are still being made to this day. They sell very well overseas I believe, where they don't go in so much for fitted carpets. The hot countries especially. Those with marble or stone floors.'

'You certainly know your subject, if I may say so.'

'I was always interested in what was going on and Raymond would talk for hours about it. I still take an interest — when I can.'

Collecting the cups from Pat and myself she took the coffee tray out to the kitchen. I stood up and looked at the immaculate garden through the window.

'This is a nice house,' I said as she walked back in. 'Have you lived here long?'

'We bought this when Raymond sold the rug company. We had a flat before but we thought this would be better for the children.'

'Children?' said Pat, enquiringly. 'Do they still live with you here?'

'No, they're not here now.' Her voice was so quiet, it was almost a whisper.

'They live away?' Pat asked. 'With their father?'

Beryl Flyte went over to a side table

and brought back two silver-framed photographs. She handed one to Pat and said:

'That was the eldest. My son. But he died. This one is my daughter.'

Pat looked at the photographs, then handed them to me. A handsome, smiling teenage boy and a pretty teenage girl, with a hint of her father's roguish look, smiled back from the photos.

'Mrs Flyte,' I ventured. 'I don't want to pry, but you can see that it's important when putting this all together, to know about your children. Won't you please tell us?'

She sat down on the settee and placed the photographs on the cushion beside her. She looked down at them.

'To understand about the children,' she said, 'you've got to understand a little more about Raymond. I've told you that he was ambitious, but on top of that he had a driving force inside him. When we sold the rug company, we were really quite young and had become comparatively well off. Raymond was now a company director and I thought, when we moved here, that we'd settle down and bring up the children, just like other people do. But no, that wasn't good enough for *him*,' she emphasised. For the first time her pride in her ex-husband gave way to malice. 'He insisted that William, my boy there,' she pointed to the photograph, 'had to be educated privately, and sent him off to boarding-school. The poor lad was never happy, his reports were terrible and twice he ran away. The second time they wouldn't have him back. I persuaded Raymond to let him go to a local private day-school near here where he could be with us. But Raymond had changed so much. His early success seemed to have gone to his head. His ego was unbelievable. He used to talk of building an empire which his son would inherit one day. He used to needle and nag the boy all the time and force him to do things he was no good at and didn't want to do.' She paused for a moment.

'You see, William was basically a kind, unexceptional boy, who was a bit of a dreamer. I used to tell Raymond to let him develop in his own way and in his own good time. One day we'd be proud of him. It wasn't Raymond's way, though. He had to drive himself, William and everyone else around him. 'It's no good dreaming,' he used to say, 'you've got to get up and do things'.'

'And your daughter?' Pat asked. 'What did she think of all this?'

'Jane. She was the apple of her father's eye and couldn't do anything wrong. She'd inherited some of her father's personality and fire. She went to boarding-school and enjoyed it immensely. When she was home for the holidays, Raymond would take her off with him on his business trips to London and other places. Even to America once. They were in each other's pockets all the time.'

She got up, walked over to the window, and seemed to stare unseeingly at the perfect lawns.

'I suppose, having gone this far, I'd better tell you how William died,' she said quietly, turning around to look directly at Pat. Perhaps she derived a feeling of comfort talking to another woman.

She paused again and took a deep breath.

'It was coming up to his seventeenth birthday. He told me that some of the sixth form boys at his school had cars of their own and that he would find a small car very useful. I mentioned this to Raymond, who said he'd do something about it. We had a birthday party for William, and Raymond joined in the fun. He has a great personality, you know, when he wants to turn it on. Towards the end of the party Raymond called everyone to order and announced that William's birthday present was standing outside — would everyone like to go and see it? We all trooped out through the front door, and there was a brand new, shiny, two-seater sports car. There were howls of delight and envy from his friends — but I'll never forget the look of horror on William's face.

'He stood white and trembling and had to be pressured into the driving seat. When the party was over, Raymond asked him if he liked his new car. The boy looked at me, almost pleadingly, then said, 'Thank you, Father, but I'll never drive it. All I wanted was an old Mini I could stooge around in — not a status symbol.' Raymond threw the glass of whisky in his hand into the fireplace. He took William by the shoulders and shook him. He called him a mamby-pamby gutless wonder — and a lot more things besides. William ran out of the room. We didn't take too much notice — we were both shouting at each other by this time. Then we heard the revving of the car engine. We both looked at each other and ran to the front door. All we saw was William in the sports car, turning out of the drive-way and shooting down the road. Raymond ran towards the gate but only moments later we heard the crash. There's a T-junction at the end of the road, and he must have been doing sixty miles an hour when he went straight over it, into the trees.'

She took a very deep breath and sat down in the nearest chair.

'He wasn't killed outright. They took

him to hospital unconscious, and he stayed there like a cabbage for six months before he died.'

Her voice quivered. Her eyes filled with tears. She gazed down at her hands, nervously twisting the wedding ring on her finger.

Looking up, she added with a sigh, 'That was the end of William — and my marriage to Raymond Flyte. There was nothing left after that.'

Pat and I sat immobile, in silence. Then I got to my feet, and walked over to her.

'Mrs Flyte,' I said, softly. 'I think we've put you through enough, I'm so sorry.' I sat down.

'It's good at times to have someone to talk to. Sometimes it's easier to talk to strangers. Raymond and I parted, and then we were divorced. My daughter, Jane, went with him of course — she didn't want to stay with me.'

'Doesn't she come to see you?' Pat asked.

'No. She has better things to do with her time. I'm just the past and, like her father, she'll be looking into the future. Why don't you go and talk to her?'

'Where can we find her?' Pat asked.

'Around her father somewhere, I suppose. He's got a country house in Leicestershire. She's probably there. I haven't seen or heard from her — not even a Christmas card — since Raymond and I separated. Finding people is where you come in, isn't it?' she said to Pat.

'That must be terrible for you,' Pat replied. 'You surely must have tried to contact her?'

'Of course I have,' she replied. 'Over and over again, until I finally just gave up. I got no reply to my letters. I phoned Raymond's office repeatedly and spoke to his secretary. She wouldn't tell me anything and said she'd pass on my messages — for all the good that did. Finally, in desperation, I wrote to Raymond and even sent the letter by recorded delivery. All I got back was a stony letter from his solicitors reminding me that, as part of our settlement, Raymond had custody of Jane and that, in effect, her whereabouts were no concern of mine. No concern of mine, indeed. Can you imagine? My own daughter.'

'But surely she must have got your letters. Why on earth didn't she reply?' I asked.

'I've told you. She was Raymond's girl, through and through. His strong influence must have turned her completely against me, and she had moved on to a new environment. After all, she was probably too young to judge things for herself. She was at a very impressionable stage in her life.'

She clasped her hands tight in front of her and turned away from us, as though speaking to herself.

'That bloody husband of mine. I helped him in every way that I could, and what did I get out of it? Just this.' She indicated the room and the furniture around her. 'I know it wasn't deliberate, but I've always blamed him for William's death. Then he takes my daughter from me. God, when I think what I did for him. I've never told anyone this before, but I even helped him cheat my own brother. I see my brother occasionally, you know — but only at a distance. He still lives here, in the town. I sometimes catch sight of him shuffling around, usually half drunk, and hide in a shop or turn down a side street to avoid him. I just haven't got the guts to face him, not after what I helped Raymond do to him.'

She turned towards us.

'What happened doesn't really matter now, I suppose, and I wouldn't tell you anyway — but I've still got a conscience about it. You've got to understand that I really loved Raymond very much in those days and I'd have done anything for him. Anything. It was only later I found out what he was really like.'

* * *

Pat held my arm as we walked along the trim pavement under the trees. We turned at the T-junction at the end of the road. Neither of us said anything as we headed in the direction of the town centre. Suddenly I felt Pat shaking, and as I looked down at her, I saw the tears forming in her eyes. I stopped and put my arms around her and she clung to me and sobbed.

'That poor woman,' she sobbed. 'That poor lonely woman.'

4

We got back to the hotel in time for a late lunch, but Pat was not hungry and went straight to her room. I ate a solitary meal in the dining-room, read a newspaper in the hotel lounge, then went to my room to make some phone calls. I lay on my bed, thinking over the events of the past few days.

Late in the afternoon, I tapped quietly on Pat's door. She opened the door wearing a light silk dressing-gown. The curtains were closed as I entered, the room in semi-darkness. I sat down in an armchair while Pat stretched herself out on the bed.

'I'm sorry,' she began, 'I made a bit of a bloody fool of myself earlier.'

'No you didn't,' I replied. 'I'm the one who did that. In all my rush to stir things up, I didn't take into account what you've been through yourself lately. First your father and then recently your mother. I should have been more sensitive.'

'Come over here,' she said, patting the bed beside her. I went over and sat on the edge of the bed, and she took my hand in hers.

'It's not your fault at all,' she assured me. 'In fact you've been very helpful, kind and considerate. I suppose it was just the whole accumulation of things, and it's done me the world of good to have a good cry. After all, I am a doctor and I'm supposed to know about people, especially women.' She smiled and added: 'I've told some of my patients in the past to go away and have a good cry — now I know it was good advice.'

'I was going to suggest that perhaps you'd like to drop your part in this and go on home. I can continue probing around and I'll let you know what turns up.'

She squeezed my hand and said, 'Don't worry. I want to go through with this. Especially now. You know, I've been lying here thinking and I'm more determined than ever that Flyte should be brought to task, if it can be done. I'm quite sure that it was the stress of this horrible financial tangle that finally killed my father. Theoretically he should have lived a long life for he did everything in moderation — except work. His practice involved him in hard work, but he could cope with that. What he couldn't face was the additional nagging worry of possible financial disaster.'

'Do you blame Flyte for that?' I asked.

'Indirectly, yes,' she replied. 'The more I find out about him the more I'm inclined to think he was instrumental in killing my father. So you see, I have a really personal interest in that bastard, Flyte.'

She lifted herself up and put her arms around me.

'If anyone can get to the bottom of this whole business,' she said, 'you can — and I want to be there too.' She tentatively placed her lips on mine. At first, the kiss was gentle and tender but then our mutual attraction and passion for one another took over. Some minutes later, she released herself from me. Taking a deep breath in order to regain some composure she asked: 'Now, what's the next part of the plan? I'm sure you've been thinking about it.'

Our moment of passion seemed a thing of the past. Truth to tell, my thoughts had been more on possible bedroom activity, but her swift return to a business-like manner brought me back to a different reality.

We arranged to meet later in the bar and have a special dinner together, during which I would tell her the results of the phone calls I had made. Her mood of melancholy seemed gone, and we enjoyed ourselves that evening.

$$\star \quad \star \quad \star$$

In the morning a hire firm delivered a car for me and we motored down to the Leicester area, stopping to have a pub lunch on the way. We found the hotel where I had reserved rooms in a village outside the city, and sat in the bar waiting for my visitors to arrive.

Richard Church was the same age as

myself and we had had a lot of dealing together in my provincial newspaper days, and also later when I moved onto bigger things. I had not seen him since I had gone abroad for my Middle East tour and when he arrived, we spent half an hour catching up on the events in both our lives.

He came with a middle-aged man, rotund, with a slight stoop, who had sandy-coloured thinning hair and a straggling untidy bushy moustache. The sports coat he wore was also sandy in colour, the pockets bulging with shorthand notebooks. A heavily scuffed pair of suede shoes, covered his feet. I recognised in him the long-service, world-weary, provincial newspaper reporter. He sipped his beer happily, and wiped his moustache as Richard and I discussed personal matters.

'But Ron here is the man you want to talk to,' Richard eventually said. 'We two could go on gossiping all night. From what you said on the phone, you're delving into the background of Sir Raymond Flyte. Ron here is the man for you. He goes back to the year dot in this neck of the woods and what he doesn't know about local events, you could write on the back of a postage stamp.'

'What is it you want to know?' asked Ron, wiping his moustache after another swig of beer.

'I'm looking into the whole of Flyte's life history,' I replied. 'We've been up North where he came from and found what we could about him there. I gather that he moved down to this area some years ago.'

'Flyte's story, eh?' he chuckled.

'Do you know why he came here in the first place?' I asked.

He thought for a while.

'It was the electronics company that first brought him here. He'd just bought it. I interviewed him at the time and he said there was going to be a big future in computers. It was some time ago when computers were in their infancy — not like today when even school kids have got them at home in their bedrooms. He took over a company that had been lurching along, with some bright boffins in charge. You know the sort. Lots of bright ideas, but no business acumen. They needed someone like Flyte to sort it out, and by God they got him. He went through that place like a dose of salts.

'After he'd got his feet under the table and got the feel of things, he sacked twenty men two weeks before Christmas. When I heard about it, I went to see him. I asked him why it was necessary to wield the axe at that particular time of the year. He didn't seem to take my point — just said that the factory was overmanned and had got to shed surplus fat. He may have been lucky that the men were not union members. I persisted and asked him why he couldn't have waited until after Christmas, so at least the men and their families could have enjoyed the holiday, and he gave me a lecture on business economics and finished up by saying he wasn't running a charitable institution.

'That's how I first met him. It was a small factory then, but now it's grown into one of the biggest.' Ron took another drink. Then he said: 'Of course, you know he made most of his original money out of chickens.'

I was not quite sure what he meant. 'Chickens?' I queried. 'Are you joking?' I asked.

'No, I'm deadly serious.'

'Textiles,' I laughed, 'I can understand, and electronics and computers — but why chickens? What sort of chickens?'

'Oh, chickens fit into the pattern all right. Flyte was always a man to see ahead and to seize opportunities. You young things,' he said, waving a hand at us around the table, 'take deep-frozen chicken now for granted, as a normal part of everyday life. The cheapest meat there is, some say. There was a time, though, when the only chickens you could buy were the sort that walked around the farmyard. People bought them from the butchers and fishmongers and only the wealthy could afford them. The Americans were the first to start the factory farming of chickens. It caught on over here but in a small way at first. There was a young chap around this way, called Ian Welling, who started up a broiler house, as they were known, with five thousand chickens. He did so well that he put up another house for another five thousand. He was a graduate from some agricultural college, who saw a big future potential in factory farming, and he wanted to expand.

'Then he met Raymond Flyte, who went into business with him, after visiting the United States to see how they did things there. All went well at first, the business expanded dramatically, Flyte got control and eventually Welling found himself out in the cold. He's a farm manager now over Sandthorpe way — I can give you his address, if you want it. Flyte apparently made a fortune out of the business. That's when he moved into Grange Manor and became one of the landed gentry. It's a lovely old Elizabethan house about five miles from here. He had a big house-warming at the time, and I was sent along to cover it.'

'Does his daughter live with him?' Pat asked.

He looked surprised for a moment.

'You don't know the story about her, then?'

We shook our heads.

'She did live with him there and became part of the local young-moneyed set. A very pretty, attractive girl, she was — full of life. She got herself into one or two scrapes. Nothing serious, until all of a sudden she got mixed up with drugs, and I don't just mean smoking pot. There was a police raid on a house where some young chaps lived, and Flyte's daughter was found, stoned to the eyeballs on heroin. She was only sixteen at the time so she went in front of the juvenile court. She got a good lecture apparently and a conditional discharge. About six months later though, by that time she was seventeen, the police found her at it again. This time the case made big headlines locally. Now, it would make the nationals, with Flyte being the big man that he is. He didn't turn up in court himself, but the girl was legally represented of course. The court naturally took a serious view and a Probation Officer was asked to examine

120

her circumstances and her background, although everyone around here knew who she was. He reported to the court that the girl had been going through an emotional crisis, and the outcome was that she was put on probation, provided she went into a medical home to have proper treatment. The solicitors representing her said that appropriate arrangements had already been made — which the court approved.

'Since then, nobody seems to have heard of her. She's just dropped out of sight. Perhaps she's learnt her lesson — I hope so, she was a lovely girl. Very like her father in looks.'

Richard Church looked agitatedly at his watch and Ron got quickly to his feet.

'We've got to go,' said Richard. 'I promised Ron I'd get him home in reasonable time. Get in touch if we can help you further.' Without further farewell they left.

* * *

In the morning we found our way to Grange Manor, stopped the car by the tall wrought-iron gate and looked down the tree-lined drive to the creeper-covered old manor house. Sheep grazed in the parkland and we could see the neatly trimmed hedges and the beautifully kept ornate gardens that surrounded the house.

We drove further on to the farm, near Sandthorpe, where we were to find Ian Welling. As we entered the farmyard, we noticed some men, grouped around a tractor. The man issuing instructions came over to us and I introduced myself and Pat quickly explained our reasons for wanting to talk to him. He was a smallish, open-faced man in his forties, rather shy in manner. He took off his cap as I told him the gist of Ron's conversation the previous evening. He idly kicked the front tyre of the car as he digested all that I had said.

'You're from the press you say?' He had a pleasant voice. 'I don't know that there's anything I want to talk to you people about. It's all water under the bridge now — one lives and learns.'

'I'm not from the press,' said Pat. 'I'm with Mr Roberts because he's trying to find out about Raymond Flyte. That man's responsible for something nasty that happened to my family. It would be a great help if you would talk to us.'

'You needn't worry about our using your name, or anything like that,' I added quickly. 'Anything you tell us won't be attributed to you. We protect our sources of information.'

Ian Welling continued looking down at the front wheel of the car as he tapped it with his foot.

'He's a big man around here now, you know. I wouldn't like to cross him. He knows too many people, and the company who own this farm along with them. Still, I can't see any harm in talking to you if you promise to keep me out of it. You could find out anyway from other people if you'd a mind to it, and I suspect you have.'

'I've got some tackle to take down to the village later. Out on the Bletchbury road there's a pub called the Hare and

Hounds. I should be there about twelve-thirty. I'll see you there, if you like.'

He placed his cap back on his head, and walked back across the farmyard.

* * *

We were seated well away from the bar when Ian Welling came into the pub. He had a brief word with the landlord before he joined us. I got him a drink and ordered a plateful of sandwiches.

'From what you've told me already,' he said quietly, 'you know that I started off with broiler chickens when I left college. I thought there was a big future in them, and I've been proved right. Now it's a flourishing business and the big boys have taken over. Everyone's used to buying frozen chicken now. In some places I believe even the milkmen deliver them. They're very cheap too, as meat goes. It wasn't always the case.

'It's funny when you think about it. Nowadays we get people coming to the farm wanting to buy free-range chickens. They're almost a thing of the past. I

124

wasn't the only one, of course, to see how things were going to change.

'At the time, a friend of mine hatched and reared the young chicks, before they came to me. I then fattened them up before sending them to a chicken-packing station. It was all a bit Fred Karno and amateurish, but it worked, and we all made a decent living out of it. I wanted to expand further but I hadn't the money, and the banks looked upon it as a bit risky. Then Raymond Flyte appeared on the scene.'

He paused and picked up one of the sandwiches and ate it hungrily before continuing: 'Flyte told me he'd been across to the States to assess the broiler-chicken industry there, and had come back impressed.' He gulped down half the contents of his beer glass. 'He talked knowledgeably about it and agreed with me that it had big growth potential. He told me that he didn't want to get personally involved — but that he'd put money in as an investment for the future. I was delighted and frankly at that time, I really liked the man. I mortgaged the land I owned to him to give him security, and I didn't think much about it. Everything was going well.

'For about a year and a half I ran things on my own. Then he phoned me one day and said he wanted a meeting. He brought along an accountant with him and he sounded off about 'vertical integration'. I didn't know what he was talking about and told him so. He got the accountant to spell it out: how much we were paying the hatchery, the packing-station for killing, plucking, and preparing the chickens and how much the wholesaler was taking for selling them. 'All that profit,' Flyte said, 'is being give away.' '

Ian finished the beer in front of him.

'He then told me that he had arranged to buy the hatchery that was supplying us, and he produced literature on the latest processing equipment for a new packing-station. I asked him where the money would come from, but he told me to leave it all to him.

'When the packing-station was nearing completion, he told me that we'd got to market our chickens under a brand name. It was new ground for me but, frankly, I found it very interesting. He told me to get on to a particular advertising agency in Leicester and to get them to come up with ideas for a name, brand image, advertising slogan — all that sort of thing. They were very helpful and arranged to bring their final proposals along for approval. I phoned Flyte, who said he'd be there if he could get away, but he hadn't arrived when the meeting started. The agency people turned up with their folders and display boards. This was a totally new game to me and I agreed to everything they suggested. There was all sorts of advertising bits and pieces, propped up all over my office.'

He paused again with almost a smirk beginning to form on his face and for a moment I thought he was going to laugh.

'Suddenly the door opened and in walked Flyte,' he continued. 'He stood looking at all the advertising material and his face went as black as thunder. There were some cards propped up on the windowledge which he swept onto the floor. 'You bloody fools,' he roared, 'can't I even leave a simple thing like this for you to do? Haven't any of you got any bloody sense at all?' There was absolute silence in the room until the account executive in charge, plucked up enough courage to ask what was wrong. 'Haven't you idiots got it through your heads that it's *my* name that needs to go on things? It's *my* name that people want to hear and see, not some fancy wet advertising name. Ray Flyte Chickens — that's what you'll call it. For a slogan you'll have — *'Everybody's Pickin' Ray Flyte Chicken'*. He went out and slammed the door behind him. Nobody said a word until we heard his car drive away.' He drained his pint and banged it down on the table.

I went up to the bar and ordered more drinks. As I walked towards the table, I noticed Ian Welling laughing with Pat. 'Everybody's Pickin' Ray Flyte Chicken,' he repeated again and now Pat was chuckling too. I looked at them laughing together and felt an uncontrollable stab of jealousy.

I placed the drinks on the table and asked, rather too abruptly: 'How is it that I've never heard of it? I think it's quite catchy.' Their merriment subsided.

'Well, now we come to the particularly nasty bit. Or at least what turned out to be nasty for me,' Ian replied. 'About two weeks later Flyte phoned me to announce that he was bringing over a couple of business associates the next day, and would I make sure that everything and everybody was on the ball? Would I also make sure that I was on hand myself? He sounded very cheerful. He arrived in his big black Mercedes, driven by one of his secretaries, plus these two men. One turned out to be Sir Hugh Laverton, the merchant banker and an MP. The other chap was German, Herr Something or other — I never did catch his name. Flyte and I showed them around the broiler houses and we explained the whole process to them. Then we took them to the packing-station, which hadn't started operating at the time. I was asked all sorts of questions but Flyte answered most of them — he really knew what was going on, that chap. In the brief conversation I had with the German, who spoke perfect English, I gathered that he was something to do with hotels and catering. They stayed for about an hour and then drove off. About a week later I received a message that Flyte wanted to see me in his office at the electronics factory.' Ian Welling took a deep breath.

'I was ushered into his office and there was this accountant that I'd met before, and someone he described as one of his solicitors. I then saw Flyte at his hyper-efficient ruthless best. Believe me, he didn't muck about. He told me that for reasons that were no concern of mine, he was disposing of the chicken broiler houses, including the hatchery and the packing-station. He pointed out that he had financed the expanded business and that, apart from the mortgaged land, I had no financial interest. He said that he was calling in the mortgage on the land. He offered me a price for my share of the buildings and the land, and he added, as if he was being generous, that he would pay me a sum of money for any inconvenience caused. He gave me a letter confirming the terms and another that notified me that an emergency directors' meeting had been held and I had been voted off the board. A cheque was attached for salary up to the end of the following month. In the first letter it stated that, if I did not accept within seven days, then the offer of so called 'inconvenience money' was forfeit.' He drank some more of his beer.

'I took legal advice of course, and the upshot of it was that I was advised to accept what I'd been offered. It appeared that I hadn't got much hope of fighting him. So that was the end of me and Raymond Flyte. In a way I was quite lucky. I didn't actually lose any money, once it was all sorted out. I just ended up with what I'd started with. I learnt the lesson, though, of not getting involved out of my depth. Now I'm a happy farmer, doing what I'm good at, and know about.' He smiled.

'But what happened to that business

of yours — the buildings and the land?' I asked. 'Why did he do it?'

'I can only tell you what I put together afterwards. You know this vertical integration talk of Flyte's. It seems that he'd got this idea of a chain of takeaway fast-food outlets throughout the country, selling chicken only or portions of chicken — another idea he'd picked up in America, and a brilliant one too. Nobody was doing it here, then. Sir Hugh Laverton, the financier, the German hotelier, who I gather had access to money too, and Raymond Flyte, put the whole thing together. They bought out a large number of suppliers and built a huge processing plant. Then they set up the famous Mother Hen chain of cooked-chicken outlets.'

'And that's what he used your old place for?' Pat asked.

'God, no. That was all bulldozed flat years ago, and they built a huge regional depot for frozen chickens there, where they store millions of them now. All ready to be thawed and cooked.'

'Don't you feel bitter in any way?' I asked.

'No. What's the use? I learnt something. Particularly to keep out of the way of the Raymond Flytes of this world.'

'Then he moved into Grange Manor?'

'Yes. It all happened about that time. He bought the manor house and initially used part of it as the head office of Flyte Enterprises. Some tax dodge, I suppose. Now it's just his private country retreat. A chap I know works for him, managing the estate. He says that they get on all right, in fact he doesn't see much of him. Things seem to be very quiet since he got married again. It's all much more respectable now.'

'He had a daughter — Jane. Do you know what became of her?' Pat asked.

'No. I used to see her, very occasionally. There was trouble with her and drugs I believe, although I don't know much about it.'

We all sat quietly for a moment, each one of us reflecting on yet another incredible account concerning Raymond Flyte's business life. Eventually Ian

Welling rose from the table.

'Well, it's been nice talking to you. In a way I've enjoyed it. It's made me realise how lucky I am now.'

He shook us both by the hand before saying, with a twinkle in his eye, 'Don't forget. Everybody's Pickin' Ray Flyte Chicken.' And chuckling he went out.

★ ★ ★

'That was one man at least,' said Pat, 'who doesn't seem to have become mentally or physically scarred by his involvement with Flyte. He seems to have come out of it as the amused philosopher.'

'More credit to him,' I replied. 'You'll have noticed how everybody seems to speak of Flyte in the same way — as a hard, ruthless, egotistical man, but with considerable personal charm.'

'Yes,' said Pat thoughtfully, 'but up to now we've only talked to people he could dominate. I wonder what happened when he started getting involved with hardened businessmen like the merchant banker and the German hotelier?'

'Presumably they were impressed by his foresight and driving business acumen. They'd be interested in only one thing — financial profit,' I replied.

'Maybe we'll find out as we go along,' said Pat. 'People like that aren't taken in so easily as the sort of people we've talked to so far.'

When we got back to the hotel, I was given a message to phone Henry Lust at the London office.

Immediately I dialled Henry's number. I knew he would only try and contact me if he'd got a good lead.

'Tony, my boy,' he said when eventually I got through. 'What are you doing in the depths of the country? You've no idea the trouble I've had tracking you down.' His voice changed to his more serious professional tone. 'Am I right in thinking that you've been following that runny nose of yours?' he asked.

'Yes,' I replied. 'I've done nothing else since I last saw you.'

'Good. Hold the line a minute.' There was a pause and I could hear him talking to someone at the other end. Then he came on again. 'I've got your boss Bill Travis with me. Even in these undisciplined days some of us do manage to observe a modicum of protocol. He's quite happy for me to talk to you. Have you found out anything about that man your lovely lady friend was anxious about?'

'Quite a bit. In fact I've just put another piece of the jig-saw puzzle together.'

'Is it interesting?' he asked.

'Very,' I answered. 'In fact he's nothing more nor less than a bastard.'

'Listen,' he said. 'Could you come in tomorrow morning to tell us all about it. There are things going on here that might make what you've been up to very relevant.'

'Certainly,' I said. 'On one condition. That I can bring my personal assistant along too.'

'Your personal assistant. What the hell are you talking about?'

'Pat Sheriden. She's with me.'

Henry gave a knowing chuckle.

'All right,' he said at last. 'Ten o'clock. And tell your personal assistant that I'm going to give her a fatherly talking to.' He added, 'In truth, I'm as jealous as hell.'

5

At 9.50 the following morning I walked into the office of Bill Travis. The room had its usual tobacco-impregnated air, but Bill had not yet arrived to add to the nicotine quota for the day. I scribbled a note and left it on his desk, and Pat and I went along to Henry Lust's office.

He was deep in conversation with the man I recognised as his assistant City Editor, and he continued talking as we walked in. I knew better than to interrupt; the expression on his face told me that this was not one of his occasions for friendly banter. I signalled Pat to a seat at one side of the room. Eventually, Henry turned to us as his companion left the office.

'We've got a flap on, Tony,' he said to me, and, turning to Pat, added, 'that means a red alert in modern-day space language. I'm sorry to appear pre-occupied, but that's the way it has to be on these occasions.'

'Don't worry,' Pat replied. 'I'm a doctor — it happens to us, too.'

'Of course,' he acknowledged. 'The reason I asked you to come in,' he said, addressing both of us, 'is that things have been happening in the last couple of days, involving our mutual friend 'Top' Flyte. We've been getting signals, smoke signals would be a better expression, that he's up to something big, but there is nothing our various sources of information can put a finger on. They've been delving hard but Flyte has been covering his tracks well. We have been able to follow up some rumours, but it looks as though they were deliberately planted to keep us off the proper scent. However, today is the day when all will be revealed. It's known that Flyte and the directors of Flyte Enterprises are to have a meeting with the board of FIG — the Felix Industrial Group. There's going to be a joint press announcement sometime after lunch. The whole thing smells of a takeover by Flyte Enterprises of Felix Industrial. Does this mean anything to you?'

I shook my head.

'I'm not going to spell it out in detail, I haven't time, but let me just say that it would be a very logical step on Flyte's part and, by God, he's been clever if he's arranged it. Flyte's group has a broad spread of company interests that encompass textiles, electronics, engineering, food outlets and hotels, among other diversifications. It's a big and successful group in its own right, of course. FIG is involved with electronics also, but its engineering interests are largely in the oil-equipment side because they have oil interests in the North Sea. They also have shipping, which includes oil tankers, freight and holiday cruise liners.

'They are bigger than Flyte in terms of market capitalisation, but there might well be sense in bonding both their overall interests together — if it can be done. The amount of money needed for Flyte to get control of Felix Industrial is huge, and that kind of money doesn't come from merchant banks alone. The main clearing banks would also have to have a finger in the pie, plus the big institutional insurance companies. This would be one of the biggest mergers of interests that has taken place in this country for a very long time.'

'How sure are you about what's going to happen?' I asked.

'I'm not. That's why I wanted to know if you'd heard something. In any case the Department of Trade and Industry is going to have to give the go-ahead, but take it from me, one gets to know the signs and symptoms when something like this is in the offing. If, as we suspect, there is going to be an announcement of a merger, then we've got to be prepared for a big story. You've experience, Tony, of what that entails.'

Pat was about to say something, when Henry interrupted her.

'Before you say anything, Pat, let me also add that we have to decide whether we, as a newspaper, think that such a merger should take place. Is it in the interest of the shareholders, and also in the public interest? In other words, what policy line and editorial comment do we make? The Editor-in-Chief is the man here who decides that, and no doubt he will talk the situation over with the proprietor, Lord Kloof. But he'll want a report from us.'

He picked up a telephone and asked for a tape-recorder to be brought in. When it was on the desk in front of him, he said:

'You two have been delving into Flyte's past, and what you have to tell us may, or may not, influence how we handle the matter. In any case we'll have some advance information about him that our competitors won't yet have collected. You said he was a bastard — now's your chance to prove it.'

He pressed the start-button on the recorder and the tape began to whirl.

I reminded him of Flyte's involvement with the McNab Brown McNab tax avoidance scheme which had started us on the track in the first place. I led onto the conversation with the Middlehurst solicitor, whose clients had similarly been involved. I explained Flyte's early life and how he had started in business with the partner he later tricked. I moved on to recount the disclosures given to us by Flyte's ex-wife, and then summarised what had developed when we had visited the Leicester area.

'We haven't finished our enquiries by any means,' I ended by saying, 'but that's the point we'd reached when you asked me to come here today.'

Henry switched off the machine and sat quietly for a time, apparently in thought.

'You certainly seem to have raked up some interesting material about him,' he said eventually. 'Whether it's enough, I'm not sure of at this stage. I want someone else to hear this.' He grabbed the tape-recorder and headed for the door. From a side-table he picked up a heavy glossy brochure and threw it to me on the way out.

'Have a look through this in the meantime,' he said. 'I shouldn't be all that long. Ask my secretary for some coffee.'

I drew my chair close to Pat's and we looked at the coloured brochure of the last published annual report and accounts for the Flyte Enterprise Group. It had been well prepared by an advertising agency and on the inside page was a large photograph of Raymond Flyte, behind a desk, looking like a man of big business. His smooth dark hair was brushed well back, and there was a confident smile on his face. The next page was headlined '*Expansion is our Watchword.*' Underneath was a brief statement concerning the past year's results, and comment on further activities in the year ahead. We noted, among the list of directors on the main board, the names of Sir Hugh Laverton, MP and Herr Willhelm Muller, MEP. A fold-over section listed all the companies and their activities in the form of a family tree, and there was further comment about each of them. There were pages of summarised balance sheets which ended in a page of condensed results for the whole group. We went through the booklet more than once commenting on points of special interest, and then put it on Henry's desk with Flyte's picture turned uppermost.

Henry came back into the room and grinned when he saw the picture.

'Been assessing the enemy, have you?' he asked. 'I believe generals did that in the war — had pictures of their opposite numbers on the walls of their caravans or headquarters. Probably trying to get into their minds to assess what their next moves might be. Now your next move is to come with me to see our Editor-in-Chief. I've been playing him your tape and he wants to see you both.'

We followed Henry up a flight of stairs to the office of Hamish MacLeod. He was a tall slim man of about fifty years of age. He was admired and respected by all those who worked on Fleet Street. He greeted us with a quiet smile.

'This would be Dr Sheriden, no doubt,' he said, in his strong Scots accent, shaking her hand. 'It's good to see you too, Tony, after your Middle East travels. You must have lunch with me and tell me all about them, but now, I'm afraid, we've got something else on our minds. Please sit down,' he said, waving us to a circle of chairs at the side of the room.

'I've listened to the tape and I find it very interesting. Very interesting indeed. I realise that this is only a condensed version of the story you've unearthed, so I've arranged with Henry that you'll spend the rest of the day expanding on it with every bit of detail that you can remember.' He added, turning on his Scottish charm, 'If Dr Sheriden has a mind to help you, then it would be our privilege to have her gracing our offices.'

He smiled at Pat.

'You'll realise, as I understand Henry has already told you, that many men who reach the higher ranks of commerce or industry, are no more than rascals. I sense though, that we have in this man Raymond Flyte, something more than just that. Henry, will get his people working on whatever we can dig up, now that you two have gone this far. But I think we need something bigger if we are to be certain of discrediting him totally.'

He turned to Henry.

'I have an instinct that the answer to

what we want may lie with his daughter. At the moment she seems to be something of an unknown quantity. Peter Dunn, our crime editor, has contacts all over the place on both sides of the law. Get him and his people working on it to see if she can be traced.'

He stood up and held out his hand to Pat.

'I'm very glad to have met you, Dr Sheriden,' he said courteously. 'I've no doubt I'll see you again. Thank you for the help you have given us.'

We followed Henry out of the room and down the stairs.

'You see what you two bright sparks have started, don't you?' said Henry with a laugh. 'When the old man gets the bit between his teeth about something, there's no holding him. Heaven help Sir Raymond Flyte if Hamish MacLeod is right — he'll really destroy him.'

* * *

After an early lunch I found an office and dictated into a tape-machine the full details of all we had uncovered concerning Raymond Flyte. It was a very much fuller version than the amended account I had previously given to Henry Lust. I interrupted a meeting to hand the completed tape to Henry, and I heard him make arrangements for their immediate transcription.

On our way out, I called into Ben Travis's office. He was deep in conversation on the telephone, surrounded by a cloud of cigarette smoke. A secretary was seated in front of his desk. He covered the handset momentarily and just said, 'Hello you two. Well done. Keep in touch.' And continued with his conversation as if we had not interrupted.

We walked out into the street, sharing a sense of anti-climax: having taken things so far concerning Raymond Flyte, they were now no longer anything to do with us. Others had taken over.

We bought the early edition of the evening paper from a news-stand. The banner headlines read: '*FLYTE — FIG MERGER*'. We stopped and read the report. It was little more, at that stage, than a basic press release with a few added comments. A smiling picture of Raymond Flyte dominated the front page.

'You've got to give him best when it comes to looks,' I remarked.

'Wickedness does not necessarily show in a person's face,' Pat replied. 'It would help us all if it did.'

* * *

We had dinner at a small restaurant that I hadn't visited for years, and talked about practically everything — except Raymond Flyte. It was almost as if, by mutual consent, he was a subject that we had agreed to steer well clear of. After our meal we sauntered down Oxford Street, looking in shop windows, Pat linked her arm through mine, like dozens of similar couples. While standing looking in a particular window, admiring the colourful display, I became aware of the reflection of another face looking at us. Suddenly, I realised who it was and spun round.

'Fred,' I said. 'Look, Pat. You remember Fred, don't you?'

'Of course,' Pat replied. 'How are you, Fred?'

He didn't reply but stood there as if he was almost too embarrassed to speak. His eyes darted over our shoulders and he looked around nervously.

'Good evening, miss, and you, sir,' he said. He glanced around again. 'I heard you were looking for someone, sir — I might be able to help you.'

'Who would that be, Fred?' I asked.

'Top Flyte's daughter. The word's out that you people want to talk to her. I might know where she is.' He once again looked nervously around. 'I'm not certain, mind you, and I was going to check before I contacted Mr Lust. Seeing you here, though, I thought I'd have a word with you first. Are you interested?'

'You're dead right we are. Where is she, Fred? It could be very important.'

'I'm not certain, mind you, and I don't want to mislead you.' He paused. 'Would it be worth twenty quid if I told you?'

'It may be if you're right. Now, come on. What's this all about?'

'It's not strictly my line of country — the city area's more my beat, as you know. With all this talk in the evening papers though, about Flyte, I've been hearing things. His daughter is supposed to be working in a night club as a hostess. Doesn't use her own name, of course. She calls herself Jane Grey. It's a night club called the Green Pastures, off Curzon Street, in Mayfair. It used to be called something else, but you know how these places change hands.'

'And she's a hostess there? Are you sure?'

'No, I'm not sure, sir, that's what I've been telling you. Just gossip I heard in a pub tonight.'

Realising that he would say no more I took out my wallet and gave him two ten pound notes.

'If you're right, there may be more for you, but mind you keep this to yourself.'

He took the money and nodded politely to both of us, before rapidly disappearing among the crowds.

Pat and I watched his retreating figure.

'Hostess in a night club . . . ' Pat asked in a slightly confused voice. 'What on earth is Flyte's daughter doing working in a place like that?' She looked at me quizzically.

'I think we can both guess at the answer, don't you?' I replied. 'Another name to be added to the files for prostitution and drug addiction, I suppose.'

A grim expression formed on Pat's face. It was not something she hadn't come across before . . . working as a doctor in the Middle East, drug addiction was all too common. But being familiar with the facts never made it any easier to accept.

Sighing Pat linked her arm through mine again, as if she needed the security of physical contact. 'Let's get back,' she muttered, almost to herself.

I waved down a passing taxi and we returned to our hotel in Park Lane. I had a talk there to the night porter and learnt from him that I would have no difficulty in getting into the Green Pastures. In fact, he telephoned and made a table reservation for me. Pat wanted to come too, but I soon convinced her that this was a job for a man, on his own; that is if it was anything like the club I'd previously known there, her presence would be a positive hindrance.

We had a couple of drinks together in the bar of the hotel, and at about eleven o'clock I set off to the night-club. The sign outside had been changed, the colour scheme also but I immediately recognised it as the same place I had known under another name. I had enjoyed some hectic nights there in the past. When I descended to the main club area below street level, I found that, as it was early for nightlife, very few tables were occupied. My reserved table was on the dance floor level. I gave the head waiter a tip and was moved to a table that was in a raised portion overlooking the whole room. The band were playing to one side of the dance floor. At the far end of the room a number of smartly dressed girls were seated together, gossiping, taking advantage of the lack of customers. The lights were dim, giving the place an air of tawdry seclusion and intimacy.

'Will you be dining alone, sir, or would you like me to arrange some company for you?' the head waiter asked.

I tried to look as if the idea of company had not previously occurred to me. I replied by asking what time the cabaret came on. He told me about one o'clock

'Perhaps some suitable company would be pleasant,' I said, lightly. 'A friend of mine has mentioned a girl named Jane Grey. Is she here tonight?'

He looked down towards the far end of the room.

'I'm not sure that she's arrived yet, but I'll see that she comes straight to you when she's here.'

I ordered a bottle of whisky, some soda, and a bucket of ice. I sat there listening to the music, watching the few dancing couples on the tiny dance floor, sipped my drink and waited. A group of men came in — sales managers, I thought, having a fling after some convention. A number of tables were hurriedly pushed together and girls from the far end of the room quickly joined the party. The place was filling up. I saw one of the waiters at the far end speaking to a girl as she came in through a far door, and gestured towards my table.

It was too dark to make out her features but I watched her as she made her way between the tables, occasionally stopping to speak to someone. When she finally climbed the few stairs towards me, I was in no doubt that this was Raymond Flyte's daughter. She was of medium height and slim and walked with the cool elegance of a fashion model. Her close-fitting black dress accentuated the paleness of her face even in the half light, and her perfectly groomed sleek black hair, parted in the middle, clung close to the outline of her face and curled slightly inwards under her jaw line. She looked in her early twenties. There was no suggestion here of the expensive prostitute, more the educated dinner guest at a rich man's table.

I got to my feet.

'You must be Jane Grey. I'm very glad

you could join me.'

We sat down, almost touching each other on the short padded double seat.

'I believe a friend of mine suggested you ask for me,' she said, at the same time appraising me. 'Am I allowed to ask his name?' She had a clear, educated voice.

'A friend of mine from the Midlands,' I replied non-committally.

She looked at me with the same mocking eyes that I'd seen so often in pictures of her father. 'And how do I know whether your real name is Roberts?' she said and laughed. 'But not to worry, as long as we enjoy ourselves.' She looked at me again. 'I think I'm going to like you Mr Roberts, or whatever your name is, and you've caught me on an especially good night. So let's have lots to drink and lots of fun.'

'What's the celebration?' I asked. 'And, by the way, please call me Tony.'

'Nothing I want to talk about, if you'll forgive me — Tony,' she said.

She told the waiter to bring a bottle of pink champagne and to keep the drink flowing. I knew the name of the night-club hostess game. Apart from making sure the customer had a good time, it was also their job to get them to spend as much as possible. I sensed, though, that this was not her only purpose tonight, but that she was really set on having a monumental party. We drank, we danced, we ate and she chattered vivaciously. There were times when I had to remind myself that I was not there just to enjoy myself. There would have been many occasions in the past when I would have viewed this as a spectacular night in delightful company. I was also aware that I was drinking too much.

The only moment of dissension arose when I asked the photographer to take a flash photo of the two of us. 'I never have my picture taken with a customer,' she said. 'No offence, I hope.'

She sat holding my hand as we watched the cabaret. When it was nearing its end, she took a deep gulp of the brandy that had followed the champagne.

'We can leave once the show is over,' she whispered, leaning closely against me.

'We girls have to stay until it's finished, you know that. House rules. I imagine you'll want to come back to my place but let's get the sordid business of money sorted out first.' Her voice had lost its amorous tone — she suddenly became business-like and direct. 'I'm a working girl, you know — not just a pretty face. It's one hundred pounds for an hour, or three hundred if you want to stay the night. That means out by seven o'clock. Believe me, those really are special rates because I like you, and I've enjoyed myself. If you'd been a big fat Arab, it might be double or treble that. How would you like to pay — cash or credit card?' she asked without hesitation.

I showed her the credit card in my wallet.

She gave a little gasp of delight. 'I guessed right. I knew you'd told me your real name — that makes it even better. But on second thoughts, it's strictly cash tonight,' she added with a laugh. 'Maurice, the head waiter, will cash a cheque if you want. I'll tell him. She got up from the table. 'I'll meet you up by the front entrance.' And she was gone.

I paid the bill with my credit card, cashed a cheque, and waited for her in the upstairs lobby. The hall porter got us a taxi and she gave the driver an address in Chelsea.

It was a modern block of flats, and we travelled up to her apartment on the third floor in a very plush elevator.

On arrival at the door of her flat, she inserted the key, and then turning to me, flung her arms around my neck. I sensed no pretence in the gesture and rather thought she was looking forward to our night together.

'Let's have a great time, Mr Tony Roberts. A really great time. A real ball — or a pair of them,' she added with a giggle, removing her arms and opening the door.

She switched on two table lamps in the tastefully furnished sitting-room, kicked off her shoes and headed for what I could see was the kitchen. She came back with a bottle of champagne from the refrigerator, plus two glasses.

'Here you are,' she said. 'This one is on me. Open this while I get changed.'

She went through to the bedroom. I took off my jacket and loosened my tie. I decided that I'd had more than enough to drink, but I eased the cork out of the bottle and filled the two glasses. When she came back into the room, she had on a silk robe that swung open as she walked. I could see the outline of her flimsy bra and pants underneath.

'Christ,' she said, 'some party this. What are you doing over there? Come on, over here.' She patted the settee where she sat down, and smiled.

I looked at her for a moment.

'Jane,' I said, 'there's something I've got to tell you.'

'Tell me? Tell me what? I can't believe you're a fucking queer. I can tell one a mile off.' Her voice had taken on a harsh, brittle note.

'No. It's not that. I just came here to talk to you.'

'Talk? Don't tell me that you're one of those dirty-talk types. Boy, had I got you wrong!' She took an inelegant gulp of her champagne. 'Go on then,' she said, 'talk dirty if that's what you want. It'll still cost you a hundred pounds for the hour — I should have made it two!' There was disgust in her voice.

I was sobering up quickly, but not quickly enough.

'It's not that. It's you I want to talk about.'

'Jesus Christ! Not the 'What's a nice girl like you doing in a game like this routine?' ' She almost spat the words at me as she drained the champagne.

She got up unsteadily and refilled her glass. She had had far more than enough to drink. 'What are you? Some sort of freak? You're an attractive man. We've had a great time together tonight, and I really wanted you to screw me — money or no money. Now we have to go into this great performance. Bloody hell! What's the matter with you?'

'The problem is,' I said slowly, 'I know who you are. I know that you're really Jane Flyte — daughter of Sir Raymond Flyte.'

Her glass was halfway to her lips. She suddenly froze.

'You shit,' she snapped at me. 'You fucking shit.' So that's what this smooth build up has been all about. I suppose that bastard father of mine sent you. And to think that I liked you. You lousy shit.'

With clenched teeth, she flung her glass at me. It missed, but the contents splashed all over me.

'Now listen to me,' I shouted, suddenly getting angry. 'I'm not from your father. I'm nothing to do with him. In fact I'm here to help you and, by God, I think you need it. I'm on the opposite side to your father, I know what he's done to you — and to your mother. Get it through your stupid head that I too enjoyed myself tonight. I enjoyed being with you. I think you're a lovely attractive person, who's destroying herself for reasons I can't understand. You need help, Jane. You need it now — before it's too late.'

'What can you possibly know about my mother?' The venom still in her voice.

'I was with her only the other day and we had a long talk. She's a sad lonely woman who's longing to see you again. Can't you understand that? There are people in this world who want you just for yourself — not just to use you. Just what the hell do you think you've got yourself into?'

I took a step towards her but immediately she swung away from me. For a few moments there was silence. Momentarily, I was confused . . . was she about to pass out? But then I heard it — a loud, heart-rending sob. She wrapped her arms tightly around herself and stood there, shaking and sobbing uncontrollably. Her breathing became ragged as she took in large gulps of air.

'Oh God!' she cried. 'What a mess. What a bloody awful mess!'

I realised that she was verging on some form of hysteria. Moving quickly, I picked her up and carried her through to the bedroom. She seemed to be in a state of shock. Placing her on the bed, I covered her with blankets. Her teeth chattered as if with extreme cold, her head tossing from side to side.

I grabbed the telephone from the bedside table and dialled my hotel number. I was soon connected to Pat's room.

'Listen Pat,' I said urgently. 'Don't interrupt with questions. Have you got a travelling medical kit with you?'

'Yes, Tony, but what is it . . . are you ill?' Her voice was anxious.

'No, I'm with Jane and she needs a doctor. I think it's some kind of hysterical fit, but Christ, I don't know! Can you get over here as fast as you possibly can. I'll explain when I see you.' I gave her the address and phone number.

I anxiously sat beside Jane waiting for Pat to arrive. As soon as the doorbell rang I sprang from the bed to answer it.

I left her with Jane and went through to the kitchen, boiled the kettle and made some coffee. It seemed an age before Pat came out of the bedroom and joined me.

'She's sleeping peacefully now,' she said quietly, 'but we mustn't leave her alone. I've calmed her down and given her a mild sedative. She really needs looking after for a time, until this spell is over. I suspect she's going to need more treatment.'

'What do you think is wrong with her?' I asked.

'It's too early to say,' she replied. 'Her bedside drawer is full of sleeping pills, tranquillisers, amphetamine and benzadrine tablets. God knows where she got them all. I suspect she's been downing them with alcohol too. I would think she must be in a very disturbed state.'

While sipping our coffee, I told Pat what had happened earlier and how I came to be in Jane's flat. I described the events of the night which only seemed to highlight Jane's sorrowful condition.

'My God,' Pat observed, 'wherever that man Flyte is involved we find nothing but a trail of broken, unhappy people.'

'Will she be fit enough to be moved in the morning?' I asked. 'I guess it won't be long before the Press hounds are knocking on her front door. Now that Raymond Flyte is big news, you can rest assured that we won't be the only ones who will be ferreting into his past.'

Pat thought for a time. 'I think it will be better to get her away from here. Ideally, she should stay put and have proper care. She needs to be in a hospital or nursing home, where tests can be carried out. Clamouring, bullying newspaper reporters are the last thing she needs at the moment.'

'But where can we take her?' I asked.

We both sat in silence for a while before Pat suddenly announced: 'Why not my home on the south coast,' she suggested. 'It's empty and quiet and I've got all the medical contacts I need there to get the girl on her feet. It's also a place where nobody would think to look for her.' Almost as an afterthought, she added: 'It might be poetic justice if she turned out to be the final link in the chain that toppled the illustrious Sir Raymond Flyte from his great high pedestal. I like the idea that our original enquiries about him started from there — and perhaps that's where they may finish.'

6

Pat slept fitfully on the settee for the rest of the night, occasionally going through to look at Jane. I made do with an armchair and eventually awoke from a deep alcohol-induced sleep to hear Pat and Jane talking in the bedroom. I decided not to interrupt, looked at my watch and saw that it was after nine o'clock. I went through to the small cloakroom and tidied myself up. There was a pot of hot coffee already made in the kitchen so I swiftly poured myself a cup of the steaming liquid and went through to the sitting-room, as Pat came through from the bedroom. It was the first time that I had seen her looking really tired. She slumped down on the settee and for a time sat there with her eyes closed.

'It's all settled,' she said rather wearily. 'Jane and I have been talking for the last hour. She woke up, bright as a button, can you believe? The first thing she wanted were her amphetamine tablets and she was livid when I told her I'd flushed them down the loo, along with her other pills. I think I've persuaded her to come to the country with us but it wasn't easy. Our Jane is a tough young lady — a chip off the old block in some respects.

'Just by chance I talked about her mother. She knew that you'd seen her, but obviously didn't realise that I had too — that's what really got her going, I think. I've emphasised to her why it's important that she drops out of sight for the time being. And she seems to understand.' She gave an exhausted sigh and added: 'She wants to talk to you, though.'

Resignedly I went through to Jane's room. She was sitting up in bed, drinking coffee and smoking a cigarette. In the daylight I noticed the dark rings under her eyes, and her shaking hand as she raised her coffee cup. She certainly seemed a different person from the one I had seen the night before. I sat down on the end of the bed. She looked at me for almost a full minute, puffing hard on her cigarette, obviously formulating in her mind what she had to say.

'Has Pat told you that we've been talking?' she asked stubbing out the cigarette.

I nodded. 'Yes, she said you wanted to talk to me.'

'Do you really want to fix my father?'

'That's exactly what we want to do,' I replied. 'We already know enough to convince us that he's more than the average businessman on the rampage. We think there's a far worse side to him than that, but we've got to be able to prove it.'

'And you need my help?'

'Very much, if you're willing to give it,' I answered. 'So far we've only uncovered a record of sharp business practice. What we need is something that will really discredit him. Do you know anything that would do that?'

She laughed without humour. 'By God, I do. But I must protect myself at the same time.' Always the business woman — like her father! I thought.

'Protect yourself? In what way?'

'Financially,' she replied. 'As things stand at the moment, I get an allowance from my father, provided I keep my head down. It's not a great sum but it does mean, theoretically at least, that I could give up what I'm doing and live modestly in a bed-sitter somewhere, without working or without starving. That's not my style, though, at least not any longer. I want a hell of a lot more than that. Once my father gets to hear I've been talking to you, then bang will go my subsistence allowance.'

'So you want to be paid for your information? Is that it?'

'As I seem to remember saying some time last night — a girl's got to live. Come on, Tony, be realistic. Why should I put my head on the block for you, just because you're on some moral crusade?' Before I could reply, she went on, 'Don't tell me that it's my crusade too or any of that crap. I would be happy to see someone fix my father — he deserves it, but I want my share of the take. Your

170

newspaper will make a lot of money out of it. Why not me too?'

I smiled at her.

'That's a question to which I have no valid or sensible reply,' I said. 'But how do I know that you can tell us anything that will be more than just another smear?'

'You don't,' she replied. 'But I can assure you that once I get started, the name of Sir Raymond Flyte will stink the length and breadth of this country — and overseas too. That I promise you.'

'Very well,' I said. 'How much do you want?'

She named an enormous sum and she must have seen the astounded expression on my face because she added, 'It's not just a figure off the top of my head. What I've done is to take the annual sum I now get from my father and multiply it by five. That means at worst that I could live in a bed-sitter for the next five years.'

I masked my surprise as best I could as I said: 'I'll have to get authority from my newspaper for any sort of payment.'

'Of course. I'd expect that,' she replied.

I turned round as I heard Pat coming through from the sitting-room. She sat down on the other corner of the bed.

'Listen you two,' she began, a professional tone to her voice, 'I couldn't help overhearing your conversation and I have my spoke to put into this wheel. Jane, first and foremost you need rest and medical care. When you are ready, and not before, you can tell Tony and his bloody newspaper whatever you want. But not before you're well. If you don't agree, then I'm going to wash my hands of the whole thing — and both of you as well.'

She looked at each of us in turn to emphasise her point. I was taken aback by her vehemence, but I saw the sense in her insistence.

'The first thing,' I said, 'is for me to talk to Hamish MacLeod. He's the one that's got to agree, and only he can authorise that sort of money.' I looked at my watch. 'He'll probably still be at home,' I said rising from the bed. 'I'll try him there.'

I went into the sitting-room and dialled Hamish's number. He was indeed at home and I outlined the situation to him. He did not hit the roof when I told him how much Jane wanted.

'It's not an unreasonable figure,' was what he said, 'if she really has something to say. But how do we know? We only have her word for it that it will be devastating. There are times though when one has to take a calculated risk. Look, Tony, will she agree to a guaranteed £5,000 now and the balance if we publish? She has nothing to lose because if the stuff isn't strong enough for us, her father will never know she's shopped him. But we want complete exclusivity of course — you know the way these things work. See what you can do. I'll hold on.'

I went back through to the bedroom and talked to Jane. I was astounded at Jane's hard-hitting techniques. She certainly seemed to know what she wanted and there was to be no negotiating. When I returned to the telephone, I said to Hamish, 'She's agreed but she wants the

£5,000 today. Can you deliver it to me with any papers you need her to sign? We are going to take her down to the country, so that she can have suitable medical treatment. Pat — Dr Sheriden — doesn't want her questioned until she's sure the girl's in a fit state to talk. We don't want to be responsible for something happening that we'd not bargained for. I'm not even allowed to give you the address.'

'Agreed, Tony,' Hamish replied, 'but the sooner we get her story, the better. I'll get off to my office now to arrange things. Everything should be with you by twelve o'clock. Check in with us as soon as you have any news.'

In fact it was half past eleven when the door-bell rang and I admitted a member of the newspaper's legal staff. The papers were signed and the cheque handed over.

I returned to the hotel, collected our cases, and picked up my hired car from the garage. It took us about two hours to drive down the motorway to Pat's home and for a time Jane was in sparkling form. Then she seemed to deflate and dozed for a while. When she woke she was in a bitchy and morose mood, and kept insisting that we stop somewhere for a drink. Finally, we did turn off the main road, at Pat's request and stopped at a pub, where she allowed Jane one drink only and gave her some tablets.

Pat took over completely when we got to her home, a pleasant small Georgian house tucked in its own garden. To disguise the true situation from inquisitive locals, I was supposed to be a friend of Pat's who had arrived with my cousin, named Jane Kent, who had recently been ill.

Now, all I could do was wait until Pat pronounced Jane well enough to spill her story.

★ ★ ★

For the next few days, I sat back and, supposedly, relaxed. Pat called in a number of her medical friends and they conferred over Jane, but she said nothing to me. The summer weather was good, and we were able to enjoy the sun in the garden, as well as taking occasional trips out. Even as a layman, with no medical experience, I could see the change in Jane. Her tantrums and moods of deep depression disappeared very quickly as the easy lifestyle began to take effect. We got on remarkably well together.

I made a point of buying all the national newspapers, to keep myself informed on the Flyte Enterprise-FIG Merger, which had provoked a brief uproar in the House of Commons. It was announced that the Department of Trade and Industry were looking into all the ramifications of the potential merger. The potted versions of Flyte's wife and background contained surface information only. Some editors were biased in favour of Flyte and others were against him. My own newspaper, I noted, took a neutral line.

I had made no attempt to contact anyone in my London office since my last talk to Hamish MacLeod. I knew that they must be wondering when I would have something for them. On Pat's advice I made no attempt to hide the newspapers from Jane, especially at the beginning when Raymond Flyte's name and picture were on the front page of all of them. Jane read them and then discarded them without comment.

We had been staying in Hampshire for well over a week, when I raised the subject with Pat of contacting my boss. I had phoned my parents the evening before, without telling even them where I was, and had learnt that the office had been trying to get in touch with me.

I agreed with Pat that I should speak to Henry Lust, without divulging my whereabouts. When I got through to him he was very blunt. There were no preliminary pleasantries.

'Tony, what the hell do you think you're playing at? What the hell is going on? You can't just disappear without trace. The boss man upstairs wants to know what he's spent his money on.' He sounded angry.

'Just you listen to me, Henry,' I replied, becoming heated myself, 'Jane Flyte is ill, in urgent need of medical care — and that's what she's getting, right now. The last thing she needs is harassment from Fleet Street — that's why I'm keeping her tucked away. When I get her story it will be exclusive to us.'

'What has she told you about her father? Good God, man, this is big news and you, one of our people, are keeping it from us.'

'We haven't talked about Raymond Flyte at all, and I don't intend to until the time is right.'

There was a long pause at the other end of the line.

'Listen, Tony,' Henry's voice had become softer, and seemed to have adopted an avuncular tone. 'Bill Travis and I were talking about you the other day. He was telling me about this social conscience you seem to have developed. For heaven's sake, Tony, you're a newspaper man and a damned good one at that, but you've got a long way to go yet. It's your job to report and let others decide what to do. Particularly with that toad Flyte lording it around the City. If he wins, with all you know about him, it's you who's going to have to live with that social conscience of yours — think about that.'

'Your point is taken only too well, Henry,' I replied, trying to mollify him. 'At the moment I happen to feel that what I'm doing is right. It's not my social conscience I'm talking about — it's basic humanity. Flyte's daughter has been a very sick girl, who, with a bit of luck, is being helped to overcome her problems. I'm not going to throw her to the wolves now, to be savaged. I happen to like her and I think she's worth saving.' My voice had become angry again as I slammed down the receiver and stalked out into the garden.

Pat came out of the house a few moments later.

'My word,' she said, 'I've never heard you sound off like that before. I've heard your vitriolic views on the morality of trading practices in the Middle East, but I'm seeing a new side to you.' She put her arms around me and hugged me. 'I'm quite proud of you for saying what you did.'

We walked hand-in-hand back into the lounge and seated ourselves on the sofa. As we did so, Jane came down the stairs into the room.

'You're in trouble, Tony, aren't you? Because of me,' she said in a quiet, almost childlike voice. 'I heard your conversation from upstairs — I couldn't help it. They probably heard it next door, too,' she finished with an attempt at humour.

'No. It's not because of you, Jane. It's because of the lousy stinking way so many things are done in this world, particularly in my world where all that matters is a good story that will boost circulation and create bigger and better profits.'

'Maybe a lot of the rotten things that happen in this world should be brought out into the open, so that everyone will know,' she replied quietly, sitting down in one of the comfortable armchairs. 'Your newspaper wants me to tell my story. In the process they want to stop my father and this big merger deal, don't they? I think they're right.'

'Jane, I tracked you down originally only with a story in mind, but now I'm viewing things differently. I don't like the way your father has behaved. I personally think he should be stopped. But I'm not going to do it at your expense.'

'And if I too want him stopped. What then?' she asked.

'Of course I want your story,' I replied, 'but newspapers can be very cruel, and I wonder if you can face the notoriety — whether you're yet strong enough.'

Jane looked at Pat, still sitting next to me with my arm protectively around her.

'One of the doctors that came to see me said it would help if I could talk about things and not keep them bottled up inside. I think I've got to the point where I'd like to do just that.' She paused and then, with one of her vivacious laughs, challenged me: 'Well, Tony, what are you waiting for? Go and get that bloody tape-recording machine.'

★ ★ ★

'The first thing for you to understand is that I really adored my father.' She spoke quickly and naturally. 'He was always active and doing things, and I found him exciting. I missed him terribly when I was away at school and longed for the holidays so that I could be with him. The girls at school used to pull my leg about having a crush on my father. I suppose in a way, I did. I got on well with Mum, don't misunderstand me, but there wasn't the same closeness — the feeling of being a kindred spirit — that I had with Dad. Sometimes, I used to accompany him on his business trips and he used to talk to me about what he was trying to achieve and how he was arranging things. Logically, it should have been William who went with him, but it seemed almost as if William was frightened of him. Daddy could be great fun, but there was another side. He could be a cruel bully, and this trait seemed to come out whenever he recognised a weakness in someone. That was one of the reasons he bullied William so much, and you know how that ended.

Poor William, he deserved much better treatment than he got, but I didn't see it then, of course. I do now.

'When my parents' marriage broke up, it was a natural thing for me to go with my father. There weren't any court arguments over my custody. Had there been, I would have fought tooth and nail to be with Daddy. Mum, I suppose, realised this, and I left her without a backward glance. I was going off to live with my adored father in a new place, and do exciting things with him — it was just as simple as that in my mind. I got rather pathetic letters from my mother, asking me all sorts of questions and inviting me to visit her. I would have replied to them but when I showed them to Daddy, he just laughed and tore them up.

' 'Don't get involved with your mother,' he used to say. 'She's one of the world's losers — you're going to be a winner like me.'

'Then he would take me off on some special outing or buy me a present. The arrival of a letter from Mummy always meant a special treat from Daddy. It sounds terrible, but I didn't understand at the time.'

She paused to marshall her thoughts, the silent whir of the tape-recorder the only sound in the room.

'Daddy used to say that he wanted me to know about his business plans because one day I would be part of the organisation. He used to tell me that now that women had equality of opportunity, there was no reason why I shouldn't succeed him at the top. He talked of my going to university, followed by the Harvard Business School. I was having a lovely time, and I dreamed of becoming a high-flying female business executive with my face on the cover of some glossy magazine.' She laughed slightly at the recollection.

'At the girls' boarding-school I went to, we were paired with a nearby boys' school. Our brother school it was called — and, oh brother. We shared a lot of our outside activities and outings with them. There were dances, theatre trips, coach outings to historic places — that sort of thing. It was considered healthy, as part of the growing-up process, that the two sexes should intermingle. We certainly did that all right. My first real experience was when I was fourteen, with one of the sixth-form boys from the other school. I had a crush on him at the time, I wasn't the only girl to experiment — lots of others did so too. The staff had no idea what was going on. I'd had six different boys, in various shapes and sizes, by the time I was fifteen. I'm not going to pretend about it — I just liked sex.' There was no embarrassment in her voice.

'Daddy had just acquired Grange Manor when I came home for the summer holidays. The final renovations and furnishings of our lovely new home were almost completed. The gardens had not been maintained and some specialist firm was working away, putting them right. I'd found an area of long grass behind one of the garden pavilions to sunbathe. It was a sort of sun-trap surrounded by high hedges. I was there one day with a rug, a book and a bottle of Coca-Cola, when one of the young gardeners appeared. He asked if it was all right for him to go ahead and trim the hedge. I was lying there in a brief bikini, getting a suntan, and I could tell that he was watching me as he worked. I was watching him too, and, to put it broadly, I decided I wanted him. I'd never had an adult man before and the whole idea appealed to me. I won't go into details, but it wasn't difficult to get him to stop working. To be honest, I seduced him, and it wasn't long before we were in full cry; me with my bikini off and him with trousers around his ankles. It was great.' She stopped talking for a while and then smiled quietly.

'I can laugh about it now, but what happened next was truly awful. Suddenly there was a roar of rage and I looked round to see my father standing there. He'd come around from behind the pavilion. The gardener rolled over and tried to pull up his trousers, but my father just went berserk. He raved and stormed as he kicked the man all over his body. I jumped up and tried to stop him but he pushed me away. Finally, he picked up the hedge-clippers and I thought he was going to stab the man with them, but instead he put the point of the shears under the man's throat. He told him that if he ever breathed a word of what had happened, or set foot anywhere near the house again, he'd kill him. He was shaking and white with anger. I shouted at him that it was my fault but he merely swiped me with the back of his hand so that I was knocked down. When I finally got to my feet, the gardener had gone, and my father stood there looking at me. For one moment I thought he was going to hit me again. I can remember exactly what he said: 'You bitch! You stupid bitch. If you want to use what you've got between your legs, then use it to advantage. Don't waste it on morons like him.' Then he stalked off.'

She paused again and Pat and I looked at each other. I could instantly sense Pat's concern and was not surprised when she reached forward and turned off the tape-recorder.

'Don't you think you should stop now,' she asked, gently. 'Isn't that enough for today?' We had both noticed the clenched hands resting in Jane's lap.

'I just want to explain one other thing,' Jane replied so Pat re-started the tape. 'Sitting here, telling you things like that, must make me sound as if I was a terrible person. But, to me, at the time, what I did was just an exciting experiment — a kind of adventure. You see, at home, I lived in a fairly immoral environment. It was common knowledge that my father used to take his good-looking secretary birds off to bed, and I thought nothing of it. We even laughed about it once. He said he'd got no time for anything but business, but needed his exercise — as he put it. He had one particular secretary who had been with him for some time — a very attractive divorcee, about thirty years of age. She was very smart and efficient, and Daddy promoted her to be his personal assistant. Margaret Milner was her name, generally called Maggie. Daddy started a public relations department and put Maggie in charge.

Miss 'Pubic' Relations everyone used to call her, and I mean 'pubic'. Before a new female member of staff was employed, whether married or not, Maggie would vet her for what she called 'looks and temperament'. All female employees had to be good-looking and with some sparkle about them, apart from being efficient at their work. They were paid far more than the usual going rate, but it was made clear from the start that in return, they had to be prepared to attend evening and night-time business parties, at which they were expected to be especially friendly to important company clients and my father's business associates. A lot of girls didn't want to know, of course, but you'd be surprised at the number who did. Daddy really had a way with people. Most of the women, in particular, adored him, especially the married ones. I think he brought something special into their otherwise dull, routine lives.'

Jane got up and walked to the window. Suddenly she said: 'I think I'll go for a walk now, if you don't mind. I'll continue some other time.'

I switched off the tape recorder. When she had left the room, Pat said, 'I'm no expert, but I suspect she's getting to the part that she'd sooner not talk about. Whatever we do, we mustn't press her. Let her take her time.'

* * *

That afternoon the three of us took a stroll down to the boatyard where Pat's father's boat was still lying on the hardstanding. Pat made arrangements for some maintenance work to be done on it and discussed its possible sale. We had an early evening meal, watched television and then went to bed. Jane had said nothing further about her father.

We were clearing up after breakfast the next morning when, without warning, Jane said saucily, 'Come on you two. Let's get on with my recording of the saga. Don't you want to hear the next thrilling instalment?'

Catching Pat's eye, I replied, 'Only if you feel like telling us.'

'Come on then,' she said. 'Don't let's

waste any more time.'

This was almost too good to be true, and I did not need a second invitation. We seated ourselves in the lounge and I started the machine. Jane resumed as if she had never stopped.

'For a time after my dust up with Daddy over me and the gardener, I can only say that things were a bit strained. I didn't see much of him, but whenever we had meals together, Maggie Milner always seemed to be with us. She told me that there was to be a house-warming party and that two of the guests who would be staying would be Sir Hugh Laverton and Wilhelm Muller — their names were always cropping up in the various business discussions I heard. They were to be allocated the best guest bedrooms.

'On the weekend of the party, the guests who were staying arrived on the Friday evening before dinner. I, of course, was doing my social stuff, and was introduced to everyone. I was even placed at the hostess end of the dinner table with Wilhelm Muller on my right.

I didn't like him at all. He insisted that I should call him Willy, but as far as I was concerned, he was just a big, fat German businessman.

'A lot happened the next day before the big party. I especially remember that whenever I looked around, Muller seemed to have his eyes on me. It was quite creepy. He invited me out onto the terrace to help him take photographs, sat me up on one of the low walls and slipped up my skirt so that it was over my knees. 'It's a pity to cover up such lovely legs,' he said. I was vaguely amused by it all, and just regarded him as a straightforward dirty, old man.

'The party was a success. I had some of my own young friends there too, and it was the early hours of the morning before the dancing stopped and we went to bed. The following afternoon cars were arranged to take guests out for a drive around the local area. Muller was allocated to the same car as me. We drove off with his leg pressed hard against mine, and at every opportunity he took my hand and stroked it. He was revolting, but I stuck it out without making a fuss.

'The weekend guests left after breakfast on the Monday and I practically backed away from Muller as he gave me a big rubbery kiss before he got into his car and drove away. My father put his arm around me and we went back into the house. He said what a great success the weekend had been and what a big impression I had made. I was thrilled. Things were back to normal between us.'

She reached across the table and took a cigarette, lighting it with her expensive gold lighter. For several moments she remained silent, merely watching the smoke spiralling towards the ceiling. As she leant forward to flick the ash off the end of her cigarette, she continued: 'It was about three weeks later that Daddy announced Muller had invited us to spend a week with him in his schloss in Bavaria. He said that Herr Muller had specially asked for me to come too. Sir Hugh Laverton would be going also as there was business to discuss and, of course, Maggie Milner.

'The day before we were to leave, Daddy unexpectedly told me that Maggie and I would have to go on ahead, as something had cropped up and that he would follow in a day or two. On arrival we were met at the airport and driven through a forest to this fairy-tale castle that stood on a peak overlooking the river. It was all very beautiful.

'At dinner that night there was just Wilhelm Muller, Hugh Laverton, Maggie and myself. We sat at the end of a long table in an enormous hall with stone walls, covered with enormous long tapestries. Muller told us the history of the schloss and some of the tapestries hanging there. I had drunk a glass of wine before dinner and another two during the meal. I can remember Muller talking about how I should note the different tastes of the two Rhine wines he was serving us.'

Jane suddenly stubbed out her cigarette and clasped her hands in front of her. Pat started to say something but she merely said, 'Please, I must go on.'

'First the tapestries on the walls started to blur, then my ears started to sing, and I began to feel dizzy. I vaguely heard Maggie say that she'd get me up to my room, and I don't remember much more. I must have passed out. Looking back, I think they must have drugged my wine.'

She got up and went over to the window and looked out. She was trembling slightly.

'I think you should stop now, Jane,' Pat said. 'Leave it there. Whatever it is.'

'You're going to hear this now, whether you like it or not,' Jane almost yelled, as she swung round to face us. She rocked gently backwards and forwards, her arms protectively wrapped around herself.

'When I came round I was in my room. Stripped naked on the bed with my legs wide open. Bloody Wilhelm Muller was also naked — right on top of me. Also on the bed was the naked Sir Hugh Laverton, Member of Parliament, Eton and the Guards, cheering on the proceedings. Stripped off as well was dear Maggie, who was recording the proceedings with the aid of a video camera. I thought I must be dreaming, but it was all too real. The more I yelled and struggled, the more they seemed to enjoy it. Then Muller held me down while Laverton had his go. Soon there was a full-blown bloody orgy with everybody screwing everybody else, especially me. And they were laughing all the time — bloody laughing.'

Jane covered her face with her hands and I thought she was going to cry. Pat immediately went over to her and took her hands gently in her own.

'That's enough, Jane,' she said, obviously worried. 'That's quite enough. We must stop this.'

'I've nearly finished,' Jane said, almost a whisper. 'They kept me locked up in that room until the end of the week. I suspect that the food they brought me may have been drugged. They appeared from time to time for another great gangbang. Always photographed by Maggie. In the end, I didn't fight them any more I just let them do what they wanted. I did not know very much when

I entered the room, but by the time I got out, I was a fucking expert.' She laughed. Then the words seemed to dry up and she closed her eyes.

'But where was your father?' I asked, unable to resist the question, despite Pat's look of concern. 'What happened to him?'

'He'd bloody well set it up, hadn't he?' was the terrible reply. 'He knew Muller fancied young girls and that Laverton and Maggie would go along with it too. Starting to climb the ladder of success rather early wouldn't you think? My own father had used me to his advantage. God knows what Muller and Laverton were willing to give him in return.'

The story was almost too horrible to credit, but I knew it to be true. I was quite stunned.

Pat led Jane out of the room and I heard them climb the staircase. I switched off the machine.

I was unaware how much time had elapsed before Pat's return — so immersed was I in my own thoughts.

She came over to me, burying her

head against my shoulder. I raised her face to mine and gently kissed her lips. Gradually I felt her body relax against mine.

'Oh, Tony,' she breathed. 'I need you so much. I just don't think I could cope with this horrible saga without you.' She drew away from me and sat down. 'I've given her something to calm her down. She'll probably sleep for a time.'

'Is any one going to believe this?' I asked. 'I've never heard such a terrible story in all my life.'

'You believe her, don't you?' Pat asked, surprised.

'Of course I do. Nobody could tell that story the way she has — not even a really great actress. Thank heavens it's on tape, where you can hear all the tension and inflections of her voice.'

'It's good that she's got it out of her system,' Pat remarked. 'It might help her get over the ordeal.'

'It's not finished yet, though,' I replied. 'There's still more to come, isn't there?'

'For God's sake, Tony, haven't we heard enough? I'm not letting that girl say another word, until I've consulted one of my medical colleagues. I'm only a heart specialist. I may have acquired a limited knowledge of the human mind, but with this sort of thing, I need advice. I don't know what damage we might be doing.'

'Why don't you play your medical friend that tape? Let him decide,' I suggested.

'That's just what I will do,' she replied.

7

Pat made a phone call, and later that afternoon went off alone in the car. Jane appeared quiet and relaxed in the evening when the three of us went out for dinner at a local restaurant. Nothing was mentioned about the tape.

The next morning Pat went off again and returned about two hours later. We had a snack lunch and were sitting in the garden, having coffee, when Jane said to Pat:

'I noticed that the tape had gone from the machine, and now it's back again. I suppose you've been talking to someone about it?'

'Yes, I have,' Pat replied. 'I wanted a medical colleague of mine to hear it. One of those who's already visited you here.' She added his name.

'I liked him,' Jane said. 'What did he have to say — that I'm some sort of nut case?'

'Quite the reverse, if you really want to know. He said you sounded a very balanced and controlled person, particularly having regard to the experiences you've been through.'

'Does he know that I later went in for drugs and ended up a high-class whore?'

'I told him all I knew about you when he first came to see you. I had to, Jane,' Pat added quickly, 'a medical man can't help unless he knows all the facts.'

'What else did he say?'

'Basically, that your reactions to what you've been through are quite normal and understandable. What you can be quite confident about, Jane, is that there is nothing wrong with you that won't heal in time. He also said that since we've established such a happy rapport, you are probably better off talking to us at the moment — whenever you feel like it. He did ask, however, if you wanted to see your mother.'

'Funnily enough,' replied Jane, 'I've been thinking about her a lot lately. I wanted to see her years ago, when I dropped out, but — I suppose I felt so terribly ashamed. How could I possibly explain to her all that has happened to me. It's strange, I've only known you two a short time, but you're the only real friends I've ever had. There has never been anyone else I could talk to — really talk to, that is. I thought my father was a friend, and I loved him. But look what happened.'

'It's one of the things we were talking about this morning,' Pat said. 'It's extremely common for daughters to establish a deep emotional relationship with their fathers. There's nothing wrong or unnatural about it in a normal family. Girls love their mothers too, but in a happy family the father figure is still there, whatever the feminists may say, as a kind of prop.'

'Do you want to know what happened after my sordid initiation ceremony in Germany?' Jane asked.

'Only if and when you want to talk about it. Only when you're ready,' Pat replied.

'I'm ready,' Jane said. 'I really am

beginning to feel better.'

We went back inside and Jane resumed her story.

'Daddy wasn't at home,' she said, 'when I got back from Germany, escorted by the famous Maggie. I still felt a bit doped, went to my room, and asked for food to be brought up to me on a tray. My father came to see me about nine o'clock, all smiles and in one of his buoyant moods. I didn't say anything to him at first — just let him prattle on. He said how sorry he was that he had to cancel his visit to Germany because of urgent business, and he started to tell me what had detained him. I just didn't believe him, and I suddenly turned on him: 'You bloody liar. You bloody stinking liar. You really fixed me. Didn't you?'

'He took my outburst quite calmly, feigning ignorance, and came and sat on my bed. I told him, without leaving anything out.

' 'I don't believe what you're telling me,' he replied. 'It's impossible. Of course I know nothing about it. Are you sure you're not exaggerating?'

' 'Why don't you ask your friend Maggie? Miss Pubic Relations herself?'

' 'By God, I will. I certainly will. This minute.' He really sounded angry. He used the house phone to summon her and she appeared almost immediately.

'She denied all knowledge of what I was talking about. She told Daddy that I'd seemed a bit strange and withdrawn on the trip, but thought perhaps that I was getting a summer cold or something like that. She even accused me of inventing the whole thing to draw attention to myself. She herself invented stories of what we'd done and where we'd been. It didn't matter what I said, she just kept denying it. She even suggested that she should call a doctor. Then they left me.

'I lay there most of the night without sleeping. I began to convince myself that perhaps my father hadn't really known anything about it. Perhaps his story about having to cancel his trip was true.

'The following day I had breakfast in my room and then got dressed. I knew I had to speak to Daddy again. As

I approached his study, the door was slightly ajar and I could hear him talking to Maggie. I stopped and listened for a moment, and then I leaned against the wall. I could hardly believe it.

'They were actually arranging that Maggie would get copies made of the films she'd taken in Germany, at some special studio she knew. Then she was to deliver one copy personally by hand to Sir Hugh Laverton at the House of Commons. After that she was to fly on to Brussels, where Muller was known to be, and hand him a copy, also. My father said he wanted them both to have plenty of time to study the film before their next meeting in London on Friday.

'I can remember him saying: 'I can then remind them that my daughter is under age. She won't be sixteen until next month. I have the master copy as evidence, of course, should I decide that it is necessary to institute criminal proceedings.' Then he laughed. 'I don't think we'll have much trouble in obtaining the finance we need after that. Do you, Maggie?'

'I flung open the door of my father's study. I wanted to rage and swear at him, but I just stood there. The words would not come but my thoughts must have registered in my face. My father remained incredibly calm.

' 'All right,' he said, 'so you know a little more about how the wheels of business sometimes turn. You're understandably upset now, but in a few days you'll be laughing about it. Remember you gave yourself away to the garden boy. If you're prepared to do that, what's wrong in selling yourself to a millionaire for a profit?'

'I ran out of the office and up to my room, packed a suitcase and left. I knew a couple of university students in Leicester and stayed with them. I was particularly welcome as they knew I had access to my bank account, with a large proportion of my allowance saved up. There were parties almost every night. Marijuana cigarettes were the norm, and they dulled my senses beautifully. It was then that I was introduced to heroin. Then came the police raid that you know about. I was ticked off in the juvenile court and forced to have medical treatment. Worse still, I was made to go home.

'Daddy and I barely spoke. He had made no attempt to get me back, saying I would come to my senses in due course. I mostly kept to my room, watched TV and smoked cigarettes. Then I thought I'd take a leaf out of my father's book — and use him. I started to co-operate. Very gradually the atmosphere improved. I hadn't been very deep into heroin, but God, how I missed it. I asked my father if I could have my allowance again, and he agreed. I also started taking any money that was lying about, whenever I had the chance. I bought things on the credit card that Daddy had arranged for me, and sold them for cash. I even stole objects from the house in order to sell them. And, of course, I used the money to buy heroin from a pusher I knew in Leicester. Life was bearable again.

'I fooled them for over a year and then I was caught in another police raid. I was seventeen then. Daddy engaged the best lawyers for me, and I was put on probation and sent to a fancy and expensive clinic for drug addicts. I was there for over a year.

'When I came out, I went back home. Daddy wasn't there to greet me and he'd never visited me all the time I'd been away. His centre of the world was now in London. Two days after I returned home, one of his minions appeared. He gave me £10,000 in cash and told me I was to receive a quarterly allowance, conditional upon my behaving myself, keeping out of my father's hair and doing nothing to embarrass him. I had to sign a piece of paper to that effect.

'So, I got myself a passport and took off to join the hippy trail. I had no money problems and didn't have to starve like a lot of those I met. I deliberately kept off drugs, despite the temptations, and wandered around the world, following the sun. I had lots and lots of passing love affairs. Then I got this burning longing to come back to the UK and lead a comfortable life for a change. And that's what I did.

'My allowance paid for the rent on my flat here, with something to spare, but I needed to earn more, so when someone suggested the hostess job, I gave it a try. It worked very well. I didn't have to turn up every night if I didn't feel like it. I made a lot of money and was very popular. But it's a bloody awful life really and I don't know just how long I could have stuck it.

'On the evening I met you, Tony, I had watched the TV news. Daddy was on it, large as life, laughing and joking, and talking about the new merger. That's why I was determined to get pissed that night. Oh boy, Tony, was your timing right!'

She stretched herself like an awakening cat and smiled: 'And that, my friends, is the tale of Miss Jane Flyte. Any questions now,' she asked pertly, 'before we conclude this press conference?'

'You never saw or heard from your father in person from the time you entered that drug clinic?' I asked.

'No. Absolutely not.'

I hesitated before I asked the next question.

'Jane, I believe your story — completely. I'm sure that many others will too. Suppose, though, that my newspaper decided to print it — particularly with regard to the events in Germany. Your father and the others involved will probably say it was the ramblings of a delinquent who turned to drugs. There's no proof, is there?'

She smiled, a rather self-satisfied smile.

'There is a chance that we can prove it,' she said. 'Late last summer, when I was heading back to England, I stayed for a time in Marbella in Spain. I caught sight of Maggie Milner there one day. I was intrigued and I followed her to a very pleasant villa just outside the town. I rang the door bell. She was surprised to see me, but there was no eye-scratching or anything like that. She was coldly polite and she seemed very curious to know about me. We sat on the terrace by the swimming-pool and had a drink together, all very civilised, while I told her of my wanderings. It turned out that she'd been living in Spain for some time. She was obviously reasonably affluent and I asked her cheekily if my father owned the villa. She replied quite openly, 'No, but he's helping to pay for it. It was a bit of business foresight on my part really. Some insurance in case things went wrong for me. As they did, in the end.'

' 'You mean with my father?' I asked. 'Don't tell me he did the dirty on you too. I thought you two lived in each others pockets.'

' 'We certainly did,' she replied, 'but in the end he just used me as he used everyone else. You may not believe this, but I loved him once. Now I hate his guts.'

' 'So what went wrong?' I asked.

' 'Your father moved up in the world. His money and power took him into the top echelon, and over dinner one night he told me that he was going to marry Felicity Carver. She was a well-known model from a titled family. I knew he had been meeting her, but his marriage announcement really rocked me back on my heels. He told me that, in the circumstances, it would be better if we ended our relationship. Cold and matter-of-fact. He offered me generous severance money — as if I were some old and faithful servant.

' 'I made certain arrangements over the next few days and then I went to see him. I told him that I'd got several copies of the notorious film I'd taken in Germany and that I wanted a lump sum, plus a generous pension for life. Otherwise I would expose his activities to the media and his marriage to the Honourable Felicity would be called off for starters.' '

'Hang on a minute, Jane,' I interrupted. This really was becoming the most incredible story I had ever been involved in. 'Let me get this straight. Are you suggesting that Maggie may sell her film? If she does, she'll blow her security. She'll no longer have any hold over Flyte.'

'If she can be made to believe that your paper is out to destroy my father and bring down Muller and Laverton with him, and she sees there's a positive danger that her cheques will stop because the paper has another mass of evidence anyway, she might be prepared to talk terms. I should think that if you meet her price, she may love to get revenge.'

I took a deep breath. Jane obviously had a subtle mind.

'I think we've got to the point where I need help and advice from more experienced heads than mine,' I said. 'May I go ahead and get it, Jane? It will mean letting my people hear the tape.'

She thought for a while.

'Do you know what I'd like you to do? I've thought about Mummy recently, a great deal. You two have been wonderful, but I'd like to ask one more favour of you. Do you think it would be possible for her to come down here so that we could meet again? After all, she's involved too. I'd hate it if she just heard about it on TV one night or in her newspaper.' She paused. 'It would be wonderful if we got together again, wouldn't it?'

★ ★ ★

Later that afternoon I phoned Jane's mother. She said she'd grown tired of people trying to speak to her about her ex-husband. I was not the only one digging around. I didn't want to break it to her over the telephone that I'd found her daughter, who wanted to see her, but it was the only way that I could overcome her reluctance.

'Mrs Flyte,' I ventured, interrupting the flow of reasons why she didn't want to have anything more to do with either Pat or myself. 'Mrs Flyte, I'm not after more information. I've got something important to tell *you* this time. I have your daughter, Jane with me here and she would very much like to see you.'

There was a stunned silence. 'Is she all right? Tell me, has something happened to her?' Her voice carried a hint of hysteria.

'She's fine, Mrs Flyte, now leave everything to me. I'll collect you in my car about eleven tomorrow morning and bring you down here. Pack a suitcase so that you can stay for a while.'

I started for Middlehurst that evening

and stopped at a hotel for the night. In the morning I was away early, and with Mrs Flyte in good time. She was full of questions when I arrived but I urged her to talk during the long journey ahead.

It was evening by the time we arrived at Pat's house. As I opened the front door Mrs Flyte suddenly seemed hesitant, as if she wasn't sure of her daughter's reaction to this reunion after all these years.

Pat welcomed her warmly and showed her into the lounge where Jane sat comfortably on the sofa.

At the sight of her mother, Jane leapt to her feet and for some moments they simply stood and looked at one another. Then Jane simply said, 'Hello, Mummy.'

Her mother did not reply, but went up to her and took her in her arms. Pat and I left the room, closing the door behind us.

★ ★ ★

Jane and Mrs Flyte spent the following morning together chatting in the garden as if they had never been apart. Mrs Flyte looked relaxed and happy, her face

215

having lost the sad, haunted expression I remembered so clearly from our first meeting. We all went out for lunch and it was a friendly occasion.

When the meal was over Jane said to me, 'I've told Mummy everything, and I really mean everything. She's heard about the whole sordid business. Now we want to get things over so that we can both live a normal life, so you can go ahead and do whatever needs to be done.'

'You're quite sure about this?' I asked. 'Are you sure too, Mrs Flyte?'

'Quite sure,' she replied. 'We're not just talking about a hard, tough ambitious business man or even a ruthless man. Raymond is evil — and he's got to be stopped.'

'Things will be rough for you both for a time. Perhaps very rough. Are you ready for it?' I asked.

'Don't worry about that,' Mrs Flyte replied confidently. 'It couldn't be any rougher than we've already been through.' She clasped Jane's hands in hers and they both smiled. 'Let's fix the bugger,' she said, with a conviction that startled me.

8

When we got back to the house, I went straight to the telephone and put a call through to Henry Lust. After our last conversation, I was unsure what sort of reception I was going to get from him, but he sounded in one of his breezy, effervescent moods as he said, 'Well, well, the shining white knight. The protector of damsels in distress. You've contacted us at last. I thought you were so enjoying your South Coast retreat in this glorious weather, that you'd forgotten all about us.'

'Do you mean, you know where I am?' I asked, my amazement obvious.

'Of course, dear boy. Have done all along. You don't think we'd let hot property like you, plus the accompanying young lady, disappear into the wild blue yonder?' His voice suddenly lost its bantering tone as he asked: 'Well, out with it, boy. Things are buzzing around here. I hope you're now going to tell me that Jane Flyte has spilt the beans.'

'She certainly has,' I replied, 'and when you hear what she has to say I think you'll agree that we can crucify Flyte. There are complications though.'

'Do you want to talk over the telephone?'

'No, that wouldn't do at all. You've got to hear the tape, and Hamish too.'

'You're sure you've got it, Tony?' Henry asked, his voice crisp and professional. 'If so, I'd better get the whole team together on it.'

'Don't worry, Henry,' I assured him. 'It's all there.' Looking at my watch, I added: 'Can you get up a meeting for seven o'clock with Hamish? I'll catch the next fast train. By the way, there's someone in Spain involved, who will have to be squared — there are obviously going to be legal problems. Make sure the whole team is there.'

'I'll see you at seven, then,' he replied. The phone went down.

★ ★ ★

The train arrived in London on time. When I walked into Henry's office, he simply acknowledged me with a quiet smile, took my arm and led me to the door. I followed him to Hamish's room, where there was a gathering of the senior editorial staff, plus the legal boys. As I went in, some of them acknowledged my arrival — others ignored me and went on talking. Hamish detached himself from a small group and went over to his desk on which a tape-recording machine had been set up.

'Welcome back, Tony,' he said. 'I hear you've got what we want.'

'I'll be disappointed if I haven't.'

'So will I,' he replied with a hard look. 'Get yourself a drink and we'll begin.'

I handed Hamish the tape, which he quickly placed into the machine. The general conversation stopped and everyone turned towards him as he stood behind his desk.

'I'll give you a bit of background for the benefit of those who haven't been involved up to now in the Flyte affair,' he said. 'You will all know that Sir Raymond Flyte is a successful business entrepreneur, and at the moment a giant merger is in the offing between his group and Felix Industrial. Flyte, like so many tycoons, made his way to the top the hard way. Tony Roberts here has been researching into Flyte's background and has come up with a long history of unsavoury business deals, which we might, in themselves, be able to use to discredit Flyte. We needed something really conclusive though, and Tony reckons that he's got it on this tape here. When we've heard it, I'll be asking for your views.'

'It's a statement,' I put in, 'by Flyte's daughter, Jane.'

Hamish pressed the button on the machine and the reel started turning. The office was quiet, apart from the distant noise of passing traffic, and the emotion in Jane's voice as she gave her horrific account. When she described the events in which she had been involved in Germany, the tension in the room was tangible.

After Jane's damning narrative came to an end, Peter Dunn, the Crime Editor, broke the silence.

'Is there any doubt about what we have just heard being completely authentic?' he asked.

Hamish looked at me and I replied, 'None whatsoever.'

'I thought I'd come across just about everything in the book,' Dunn said, 'but this beats them all.'

There was no expression on Hamish's face, but I sensed the anger in him. An angry Hamish was a formidable man.

'Two minutes to think about it,' he said quietly. 'Then we'll all meet around the table in the conference room.'

I helped myself to another drink, talked to some of my colleagues, and we slowly drifted through to the adjacent meeting-room and seated ourselves at the long table. Hamish came in last, took the chair at the head of the table, and looked around at all of us. There was now a grim expression on his face.

'As I've said before, some of you don't know the whole tangled web of Flyte's career. Those of us who are normally involved in these matters have had our doubts about him for some time. Is there anyone here though, who having heard that tape, thinks that Raymond Flyte is a fit and proper person to be heading the giant corporation that will come about if the proposed merger with FIG is allowed to continue? He will become one of the most powerful men of commerce in the land, with enormous and far-reaching influence. Can we allow this to happen?'

He looked down the table — we were all in agreement.

'Good, we're all agreed, then,' he continued, solemnly. 'Flyte has got to be stopped. What we have to decide now is *how*. The Jane Flyte statement, if supported by the corroboration of Maggie Milner, is probably all we need.' Nodding towards our legal advisor, he asked, 'Is it likely that criminal charges would be brought against Flyte for procuring his daughter, then a minor, in the way that he did?'

Our legal expert, James Price, played

with a pencil on the table in front of him, thinking over his reply. Eventually he said:

'Once this meeting is over I will go and get confirmation of my opinion, but it is my feeling that in view of the time that has elapsed between the offence being committed and the present time, it is unlikely that the DPP, that is the Director of Public Prosecutions, would prefer charges. There is also the possibility that because of the inevitable vast publicity concerning the whole matter, before any trial could possibly take place, it could be argued that Flyte could never have a fair trial.'

He paused.

'What have we got here? A daughter, now in her early twenties, alleges that her father, some six or seven years ago, when she was then fifteen years of age, arranged that she should have sex with two older men. She did not complain to the authorities at the time, although she had every opportunity to do so. However, she decides to do so, all these years later, while she is in the pay of this newspaper. Although the video film can prove that the event took place, it will have to be proven that she was under age at the time. Flyte will no doubt deny that he had any knowledge of the matter. Laverton and Muller, although in the film, can deny that they knew she was under age. Furthermore, they will no doubt say that what took place was entirely with her consent. The prosecution would have to rely on the word of the girl herself, who is an admitted callgirl, plus the word of a woman who was a party to the whole unpleasant affair and who will be painted as a woman of doubtful character because of her own involvement. It will almost certainly be said that she expected to marry Flyte and is out to get her revenge. She will be painted as jealous and, therefore, an unreliable witness.

'There is a further complication, I shall have to take advice on. The sexual act took place in Germany, and it could therefore mean that those concerned would have to be charged by the German authorities, under German law and tried in a German court, even if the procuring was one in England. I don't know if a Statute of Limitations would apply in Germany. It wouldn't here. The whole matter might not be as straightforward as it appears at first sight.'

'You mean the bastard gets away with it?' I suddenly blurted out, anger mounting.

'It may well be that charges will not even be brought,' Price said.

'It wouldn't surprise me to learn that Flyte went into the legal aspect, even before he set it up,' I commented.

'Are you saying that we cannot use the disclosures of Jane Flyte and Maggie Milner?' Henry asked.

'No, I'm not saying that at all,' Price replied. 'If we are satisfied that the sexual story is true, we can publish the facts as we know them. We must face the issue, though, that Flyte may retaliate by suing us, claiming that what we have printed is untrue. In fact it may be impossible for him not to do so. Maybe that's what we want him to do. That's not for me to say. But we would have the heavy task of justifying our allegations, with all the consequent risks.'

'There'd be a bloody big explosion around the name of Flyte,' Hamish commented. 'Just at the time when he is anxious to appear as a clean, healthy, man of business, instead he will be at the centre of a scandal that will rock the City.'

'And when that happens,' said Henry, 'the City doors will start slamming in his face, so fast that he won't know what's hit him. Especially those of the big institutions and the merchant banks who value their reputations.'

'Will it stop the FIG merger?' asked Hamish. 'Can we be certain of that?'

'Undoubtedly,' replied Henry. 'It will even be interesting to see if he survives as a director of his own company. His place on his own board could even be in jeopardy if the pious shareholders get the bit between their teeth, and do something about it.'

'Right,' said Hamish. 'The final decision as to whether we screw Flyte to the ground, is mine, but I must consult the proprietor. Any comments so far?'

'You realise that Flyte is likely to seek an injunction, to prevent us printing the exposure, if he hears about it in advance,' said James Price. 'He'll almost certainly sue for damages if we do print, but his first move will be to try to stop the publication altogether.'

'You and I, James,' said Henry, 'have been through a number of these situations before. We'll have to spread the exposures over more than one issue, and Flyte will certainly try to stop us after the first.'

'Indeed,' Price agreed. 'As soon as he sees it in print, he can go to a judge and ask for an injunction to prevent further publication by us of what he will describe as libel on the grounds that we have published, and intend to further publish, statements damaging to his reputation, but by then the damage will be done. From what I've heard of Flyte, he'll fight like hell.'

'The involvement of the Milner woman?' asked Bill Travis. 'How are we going to handle that?'

'That's next,' said Hamish. 'I want you, James,' turning to the legal adviser, 'to fly out to Marbella tomorrow and contact her. Remind her of her conversation with Jane Flyte, warn her what will happen if she doesn't co-operate and do a deal with her. At least that way, if we run the story, we'll have her evidence. It's an expense worth incurring because of the urgency. I want a features team with photographers to fly out with you. We've got to have her tape or a copy of it. She's got to be tied into a watertight contract to us, that nobody else can get in on. Tell her that Flyte and his empire is about to collapse and that she'd better get into our act while there's still something to negotiate. With or without her help, we are going to run this feature. Now, how much are we going to pay her?'

The meeting developed into a discussion of anticipated higher revenue on increased sales, the value of world rights for the story, media spin-off and further financial implications. A top figure to Maggie Milner was discussed and finally agreed upon, plus the possibility of a further bonus payment for her life-story rights. Overall, this was going to be explosive stuff. The newspaper looked like having total exclusivity on a feature that promised juicy reading for the international public, whose interests were far beyond the city of London. All the details of a major campaign were discussed, all with one object in view — the destruction and downfall of Raymond Flyte.

9

I followed Hamish through from his office into a lobby, at one side of which were lift doors.

'Tony, we've got to go and see Lord Kloof on this one, right away,' Hamish stated as he walked into the lift and pressed the button for the top floor.

As the lift stopped I heard the faint ring of a bell. There was a speaker entryphone set in the left wall, and a voice from it said, 'Yes, who is it?'

'Hamish, Lord Kloof.'

The doors slid back and we walked out into a large open-plan room and past an array of rubber plants and other tall shrubs arranged to form an entrance lobby. To our right was an enormous oak desk covered with neat piles of papers. There was a half circle of chairs in front of it. To our left was the dining area, and the far end of the room was set out as a comfortable sitting area, with a stone fireplace and a large portrait of Lord Kloof over it. The curtains were not drawn and I could see through the long windows to the floodlit terrace and roof garden which lay beyond them. A series of doors punctuated the wall to our left, and illuminated oilpaintings hung between them. One of the doors was partially open and a voice called out:

'Come, I'm in here.'

I followed Hamish across the deep pile carpet. He stopped before the door and signalled me to go ahead of him. I stepped through into a large, brightly lit, tiled bathroom. At the far end Lord Kloof sat in his shirt sleeves, on a large mahogany lavatory seat, his trousers down below his knees. On the table in front of him was a stack of papers. To his left stood another table covered in a variety of telephone instruments, and a console of pressbuttons. I registered all this in my first quick glance and immediately stopped, backing towards the door, mumbling an apology.

'Come in, come in,' Lord Kloof said. 'Haven't you seen anyone sitting on the bog before? What's the matter with you? Everyone shits, you know.'

I didn't reply but sat in a chair that was indicated to me. Hamish also sat down.

Lord Kloof had the reputation of being a very tough operator. This was reflected in the hard face that topped his squat broad shoulders, and his full head of fine white hair that surrounded it.

The lines etched on his face were evidence of his seventy-odd years and his numerous commercial battles. He picked up a half-smoked cigar from the ashtray in front of him with a gnarled hand. As he puffed on it, the blue smoke was drawn to an extractor fan that buzzed quietly in the wall beside him.

There was a hint of his South African accent as he said, 'I suppose you've come to tell me about this Raymond Flyte business. Well, go on. I'm listening.'

'We've got to the crucial stage,' said Hamish. 'Tony Roberts here, has come up with some pretty damning stuff, and I want to go ahead and run a series of articles but there are risks. We need to discuss it with you.'

'Damning stuff, what damning stuff?'

As Hamish started to reply, Lord Kloof intervened, 'It's Roberts who came up with the dirt, let him tell me.'

I began by relating how Pat's father had got involved in the tax-avoidance affair, but he cut me short. 'So what? I know about that and much more. He got caught when he should have had more bloody sense. What else?'

I gave him a summary of Flyte's first start and how he had tricked his partner. Then I moved on to my talk with Mrs Flyte, followed by an outline of his dealings over the poultry business, when he had first got involved with Laverton and Muller. Finally, I told him in greater detail the events surrounding Jane Flyte and Maggie Milner, with particular emphasis on the sex scene in Germany. He puffed on the cigar clenched between his teeth, listening intently, his eyes half closed. He only opened them when I came to a stop. He stubbed out his cigar and said, 'What else?'

'That's about it,' replied Hamish, 'but,

in my opinion, there's more than enough to destroy him.'

Lord Kloof made no reply, but drew from a toilet roll a handful of paper and ostentatiously cleaned himself. He stood up, pulled his trousers around his waist and fastened them. Bright red braces hung down on either side which he did not pull over his shoulders. He flushed the lavatory, walked over to the washbasin, and rinsed his hands.

Hamish was obviously used to this scene. When he was ready, Lord Kloof led us out of the bathroom into the lounge area next door and seated himself in a large armchair. He beckoned us to take nearby seats and made an elaborate play of lighting a new cigar. After what seemed like an age, he finally said: 'It doesn't seem to me, Hamish, that I've heard anything that I should risk my shirt on. As editor-in-chief you have freedom of action, in general terms, except when it comes to spending, or losing, a lot of money. Christ, man, Flyte could take me to the cleaners on this one. He'll be flashing injunctions and writs so fast they'll seem like bloody confetti. And for what purpose? You'll increase the circulation and revenue of the newspaper temporarily, there's no doubt about that — everyone wants to read dirty exposures but what about the subsequent legal costs and damages if we lose? I'll be paying those, not you.'

'But don't you think Flyte should be stopped?' I asked.

'Why?' he replied. 'Tell me why.'

I was flabbergasted. 'Because he's a man of highly tainted background who will be acquiring even further power — he's totally immoral,' I protested. 'Let him get away with this and there's no knowing what he'll do next.'

He took the cigar from his mouth and placed it in the ashtray beside him.

'Immoral! That's a word I haven't heard in this room in a long time. Christ, man! I'm not sure that it's a word I can afford to hear. My role in life, young man, is running a large commercial empire, which happens to include this newspaper. I am not here to judge morality. Hamish prints pictures of girls with big tits on the centre page because that's what a lot of his readers want. There are those who may say those pictures are immoral.

'My colour printing plant in Holland turns out girlie magazines with men and women in all sorts of strange poses. Some would say that they're immoral. It's not for me to judge. It's a matter for the people who want to buy them. Don't let us talk about morality, for Christ's sake.'

Hamish hurriedly put in, 'I'm not as concerned about the morality of the situation as the fact that I've got a bloody good story. It's too good not to run. But Flyte is an evil man in my book, and I don't care if we bring him down.'

'Using my money to do it,' added Lord Kloof, pointedly. 'Let me put this so-called evidence of yours together and see what we've got. In Flyte's early days he tricked his partner to get his financial start. The bloody fool was taken for a ride and is now the town drunk. He'll look great in court. Flyte's ex-wife tells a long tale of woe, but is heavily inflamed by the fact that her son was given a hard time by his father, and got killed in an accident. Flyte's start with the poultry business and the move into hotel and property, helped by Laverton and Muller, is hardly worth mentioning. It just proves he's a hard tough businessman; that's why a lot of people like him. His daughter gets mixed up with drugs, becomes a hippy, and ends up a high-class whore. The Milner woman is herself involved in the sex escapade and like the daughter is hardly a reputable, reliable witness against her former employer. Just think what a top-class barrister would do to them in court. He'd tear them apart.'

'So you don't agree to my publishing?' asked Hamish.

'I didn't say that. I need time to think about it. There are other far-reaching considerations to be taken into account.'

'May I ask what those are?' I ventured.

Kloof must have heard the anger in my voice.

'Yes, young man, you may; and if you

listen, you might learn something. You started on the trail of Raymond Flyte because, no doubt, you were attracted by a pretty face. If she'd been an old boot, I wonder if you'd have bothered.' His hand waved down my attempt to interrupt. 'I'm not interested in your explanations or your motives. You've managed to discover how a hard businessman made it from the bottom to the top. His career may have put a lot of noses out of joint along the way, but whether you like it or not, he has been very successful, and he's built up an organisation which now employs tens of thousands of people. Those people won't thank you for airing his dirty linen in public, if they lose their jobs as a result. This could easily happen if the financial institutions in the City withdraw their support. The coming merger with FIG is a sound scheme. It promises great expansion, and further employment in areas where it's badly needed. Why do you think the City is behind it? It's a great idea, and Flyte has worked his arse off to bring it about. Good luck to him. He may be a first class shit, but this shit is going to put people into jobs, and make money both for wage earners and investors. It's the sort of thing he's good at — can't you see that?'

'You make him sound like a public benefactor,' I replied resignedly, 'but at what stage do we stop condoning the actions of the Flytes of this world?'

'When people like me decide that the time has come to do it,' Lord Kloof replied dismissively. He picked up his cigar and lit it.

'Now listen, Hamish,' he began, 'this young man has done a good job of investigative reporting. I won't deny that. Get all the loose ends tied up and make sure everybody's evidence is on tape or suitably recorded. Sign them all up, get their consent, pay them whatever is necessary, so that we are ready to go ahead. If we decide against it, I'll take the responsibility — it'll be money well spent. I'll try to give you my answer within forty-eight hours.'

'I'm not sure we can completely bury the issue now,' Hamish replied.

'Particularly since my meeting tonight. The word will be out on the street that we're up to something. You can't stop rumours and gossip.'

'Fuck rumour and gossip,' Lord Kloof almost shouted. 'They won't cost me millions in libel damages.'

He got up from his chair and walked towards the bathroom door, saying, 'These bloody guts of mine are killing me.'

Hamish and I walked to the lift and descended to his office — in silence.

10

I got into bed at the Strand Palace Hotel in the early hours of the morning. As I tried to sleep, the events of the past weeks, culminating in the talk with Lord Kloof, kept revolving in my head. Until that meeting with Kloof, everything had seemed so clear and straightforward — now I realised it was not up to me whether we printed the articles on Flyte — Lord Kloof had pointed out factors that I had not even considered.

I finally fell asleep about dawn and awoke at 9.30, feeling rough. A cold shower helped me to get started, plus the breakfast which I ordered to be brought to my room. It was 10.30 when I walked into Henry Lust's office. The moment he saw me, he stopped dialling and replaced the telephone receiver.

'I was trying to get hold of you. Something has happened. Pat's just been on the phone and wants to talk to you urgently.'

'What about?' I asked.

'I don't know, she wouldn't tell me. She asked if I knew where you were, and said it was most important that she should speak to you. As soon as possible.'

He slipped a telephone across his desk towards me and I dialled Pat's number. She answered the phone quickly.

'Thank God it's you, Tony,' she said. 'Things have been happening down here. I didn't know what to do. I didn't want to talk to anyone else. It's Jane and Mrs Flyte — they've gone.'

'Gone!' I repeated. 'How do you mean, gone?'

'A man in a car came and talked to them, and they packed their cases and left.'

'Where have they gone to?' I asked.

'That's just it. I don't know.'

'Now wait a minute, Pat,' I said calmly. 'Take your time, and tell me exactly what happened from the beginning.'

'I'm sorry,' said Pat. 'It's not like

me — I'm a bit flustered.' She paused. 'We were finishing breakfast in the kitchen just after nine o'clock. I heard a car in the drive but thought it was the postman. Then the door-bell rang. When I opened the door, there was this man standing on the step with a big black car behind him.'

'What did he look like?' I asked.

'Pleasant looking, perfectly respectable, about forty, dressed in a dark suit. He asked if he could speak to Miss Flyte or Mrs Flyte. I asked him who he was and he didn't tell me. Just said that he'd come to deliver a letter. He handed me an envelope on which both their names were typed. I didn't ask him in or pretend they were not there. I was completely taken aback. So I took the letter to Jane and her mother.

'Jane took the letter from me and opened it. She read it a couple of times, then asked me if I would excuse them for a few minutes. They went through to the lounge and closed the door. I was clearing up the breakfast things, when Jane came through and asked me if she could take the man into the lounge for a few minutes. Of course I agreed.

'About half an hour later he went out and sat in the car. Then Jane and her mother came and told me that they were leaving with their visitor. When I asked them why, they said they couldn't tell me and were obviously embarrassed. I said, 'Do you know what you're doing?' and Mrs Flyte said, 'Yes. It's just possible that this is the turning-point!' I begged them not to do anything until I'd spoken to you, but Jane just said, 'I think it's gone beyond that point now.' They went upstairs, packed their cases, and left in the car about fifteen minutes ago.'

I asked Pat a few questions but the only additional information she was able to provide was that the car was a black Mercedes, and that she thought the number plate had the latest year prefix, but she had been too flustered to think of taking the number.

We arranged to meet that night at the Grosvenor House Hotel, as Pat felt disinclined to stay on her own in the house.

When I put down the receiver, Henry said: 'It's obvious something's up. What's happened?'

When I told him, he spat: 'That's just great! Exit, to an unknown destination, two of the star turns in the Flyte saga. You'd better go and tell Hamish right away — it puts things in a very different light.'

I had to wait ten minutes with Hamish's secretary before I could get in to see him. When I told him the news, his anger was apparent. 'Everything in this bloody thing was going too smoothly . . . Then the proprietor starts getting awkward — and now this. I sense the hand of Raymond Flyte involved here somewhere. He certainly doesn't intend to go down without a fight. This disappearing act, though, is something I hadn't bargained for.'

'You don't think he'd do something completely stupid, do you, like having them — ' I hesitated to use the word that was in my head — 'permanently removed?' I finally said.

'That bastard is capable of anything.

Obviously the word's out and he wants to make sure they're not available when we go to print. But I wouldn't have thought he'd have sent a car to collect them, if he was up to something really nasty. I'll put the word out that we're looking for the women again. Peter Dunn can get his crime boys on to them. Two women like that can't just disappear in broad daylight.'

'They haven't disappeared,' I said. 'They went willingly. They weren't kidnapped.'

'They've still disappeared as far as we're concerned,' he answered. 'Of course, we are only assuming that Flyte is behind this. It could be a throw by Laverton or Muller. Or one of our rival newspapers may have climbed in on the act.'

'I don't think Jane or her mother would change sides like that. I believe you're probably right in thinking that Flyte has got them.'

I spent the rest of the day around the office, helping where I could and putting some enquiries out on my own account. By the end of the afternoon we had drawn a blank.

I was preparing to go off to Grosvenor House to meet Pat when I got a message that Hamish wanted to see me. He was pouring himself a drink from his liquor cabinet as I entered his office.

'You'd better get yourself one too,' he said. 'Jim Price has just been on from Marbella and this is really going to throw you. He phoned Maggie Milner first thing this morning from London to tell her he was flying out to see her, on an urgent matter, to her financial advantage. She said she'd be waiting for him and was very interested to hear what he'd got to say. When he arrived at her house there was nobody there except a Spanish maid who said Maggie had gone away a few hours earlier. She had no idea where to, or for how long.'

'I don't believe it,' I said incredulously — although I did only too well.

'You can believe it all right — and there's more to come. We also know that Maggie caught a flight out of Spain about half an hour before Jim's plane landed.'

'Where to?' I asked.

'Here. To London. We know for certain that she arrived on a flight from Malaga, but where she went from the airport, God alone knows.'

'There's our third star witness gone. The one with the vital video film — and all in a matter of hours. Somebody has certainly been busy.'

Hamish and I kicked the whole thing around over another drink, and I had to agree with him when he said that he was putting a hold on the series. Whether the proprietor was willing or not, as things stood we had no feature to run. Without signed-up witnesses, under contract to us, the whole thing was a dead duck.

★ ★ ★

I noticed Pat as soon as I walked through the foyer of Grosvenor House sitting in one of the large armchairs immersed in her newspaper. My mood lightened considerably at the sight of her.

'Are you waiting for someone in particular, madam?' I asked, unannounced.

248

Thrusting her newspaper aside she stood up smiling and kissed me on the cheek.

'Oh Tony, you made me jump!' We laughed.

I took her hand and led her into the dining-room where we seated ourselves at a corner table.

'Tell me all the news,' she whispered anxiously.

'I wish there was news to tell . . . The truth of the matter is that we tried to work out what has happened and came up with a variety of speculative theories, but nothing that filled us with any enthusiasm.'

We continued our dinner trying to avoid the subject of Raymond Flyte.

With our meal over, I escorted Pat to her room. She opened the door and then turned towards me expectantly. Without hesitation I took her into my arms and we kissed passionately both recognising our mutual desire.

Slowly I broke away. I knew if I stayed any longer I would ask the inevitable question . . . What had happened to the detached reporter? I asked myself. The professional man who prided himself on always remaining distant when it came to affairs of the heart. Not any more . . . I knew I was falling in love with this woman.

But before I could make an attempt to depart, Pat clung to me again and said: 'Tony, don't go. I don't want to be on my own tonight.' And with that she led me into her room.

★ ★ ★

It was daylight when I returned to my room. After a hot bath I walked in the crisp morning air of Hyde Park, thinking about Pat and all that had happened since we first met.

We had breakfast together in the hotel coffee shop. She was sparkling and cheerful and we caught ourselves smiling at each other like two new lovers — as indeed we were. We arranged to meet again that evening and I went off to Fleet Street. Pat had to see her people at the Saudi Embassy.

At the office, I started ringing around my various contacts. I arranged to go out to Heathrow Airport to talk to our man there and I left the building just on lunchtime. Bill Travis walked down the stairs with me and we went together into a nearby pub. We talked about the latest events over a beer and a sandwich. I was just preparing to leave when Bill said:

'I suppose when this little lot is over we'll have to talk about your leave. You haven't had much so far, have you? You certainly can't count the time you've spent on this Flyte business.' His eyes twinkled at me. 'Got any plans?' he asked. 'With your new girlfriend?'

'Possibly,' I answered, 'depending on how much longer she's got here.'

'She lives somewhere down on the south coast, doesn't she?'

'Yes,' I replied. Then the import of what he had just said started to sink in. 'But you know where she lives, Bill.'

'Not exactly. I remember that it's one of the yachting towns.'

'But when I was tucked away with Pat and Jane Flyte for a couple of weeks, you

251

gave me the impression that you knew exactly where I was.'

'Only in general terms. I told people that I didn't know where Pat lived, which was true. It's Henry that you've got to thank. He was the one who kept Pat's actual address quiet.'

I said no more, but finished my beer and told him I would be around later. I took the underground out to the airport and talked to our man there. I left him a photograph of Maggie Milner, asking him to make further enquiries in case anyone had seen her being picked up. All the time I was thinking about my conversation with Bill.

When I got back to the newspaper, I went to Henry Lust's office. I walked straight in, closed the door and seated myself in front of his desk. He leaned back in his chair, a slightly quizzical expression on his face, his hands pressed together in front of him, as if in a praying gesture.

'It looks, dear boy, as if all the birds have flown the nest. First the Flyte pair, and now the famous Maggie. Too bad . . . But I'm afraid these things are sent to try us. Who knows? We may catch them yet.' He finished dismissively.

I looked at him for a time.

'I have a feeling we won't,' I replied. 'Not while someone here is passing on information about them.'

His eyes shot up. 'Passing on information? What on earth do you mean?'

'You know what I mean, Henry.'

'What on earth are you talking about?' His cool exterior seemed to have disappeared.

'I'm talking about a specific leak of information from this office to outside parties. When I say this office — I mean *this* office.'

'I haven't the faintest idea what you're talking about. Maybe that Middle East sun has finally gone to your head.' His attempt at a joke did not relieve the tension.

'You know exactly what I mean, Henry. It has to be you. Only you knew where Pat and I were staying. The actual address. I thought that Bill knew too — but he didn't. Only you knew. Last night we had a meeting to discuss our plans to topple Flyte. This morning, first thing, a car arrives at the very house and spirits away our two key witnesses. At the same time Maggie Milner is contacted and she, too, takes off. Only somebody who was at that meeting last night could have passed the information on so quickly, with details of what we planned to do. Someone tipped off the most interested of all parties — Raymond Flyte.'

'Balls,' Henry spat, now angry. 'What a lot of bull. You want your head examined. There were loads of people at that meeting. When it broke up and things started to happen, tongues were wagging all around the place. The whole thing must have been general knowledge in five minutes.'

'But,' I said with emphasis, 'only two people there knew where Jane Flyte and her mother were staying — at that moment.' I paused, took a deep breath. 'How much are you getting paid, Henry?'

We sat there staring at each other and

I knew from the expression on his face that I was right. Henry was the mole in the pay of Raymond Flyte.

A telephone on his desk rang, breaking the tense silence. He slowly leaned forward and picked up the receiver. I heard him say, 'Yes, he's here. I'll tell him.'

He put the phone down and said, 'That was Hamish. He wants us in his office at five to six. We're to go with him to see Lord Kloof.'

'I wonder if you've been found out,' I commented.

I got up, looked hard at him, then walked out, slamming the door behind me.

11

It was exactly six o'clock when we stepped out of the lift into Lord Kloof's apartment. A waiter met us and took our orders for drinks as we made our way down the huge room. Kloof stood under his portrait at the far end in front of the fireplace. I could see the back of a man's head who was seated in a high-backed winged chair. I took the drink that was handed to me, greeted Lord Kloof and turned towards his guest. For a brief moment I froze.

Kloof obviously noticed it, for he said to Sir Raymond Flyte: 'It seems, Ray, that you always surprise people. I think you know these two,' he added, indicating Hamish and Henry, 'but you don't know Roberts here.'

Flyte smiled up at me from the chair. I registered those mocking, dark eyes that had been seen so often in his photographs.

'No, we haven't met,' he answered lightly, 'although perhaps we know a lot about each other.'

He raised the glass in his hand and gave me a steely glare as he raised his glass to me in a silent, mock salute.

Lord Kloof waved us to chairs. I felt Flyte's eyes following me, but I tried not to look at him.

'Well, now,' Lord Kloof began, 'Sir Raymond and I have been having a quiet chat together — we have had a variety of things to discuss and we've covered a lot of ground. Haven't we, Ray?'

'We certainly have, David,' Flyte replied affably.

'I asked the three of you to come and have a drink with us, so that we can confirm the policy line that this newspaper will be taking concerning the imminent merger of Flyte Enterprises and FIG. So far, Hamish, you have taken a prudent middle-of-the-road line. Quite right too. However, as a result of my talk with Sir Raymond today, I am satisfied that we should give his enterprise all the favourable publicity that we can. I am very glad that he and I have had this meeting because it's cleared away, shall I say, any misunderstandings that might have arisen.'

'The fault, if any, David, is mine,' replied Flyte charmingly. Turning to us, to me in particular, he added, 'Lord Kloof and I sit on one or two committees together, but I've been so involved in this merger business that we haven't met as frequently as usual.'

I caught Hamish's eye and he fractionally shook his head at me. Henry asked one or two innocuous financial questions about the group merger.

'Are your family well?' I felt suddenly emboldened to say.

Flyte's anger at the question was obvious, but he quickly recovered himself. While studying him, though, I did not see the effect of my question on Kloof.

'Excellent, thank you,' Flyte said. 'Lady Flyte is in the country. But perhaps you are referring to my daughter and my ex-wife. Yes, they're in good form. Full of spirit.' He gave a jocular little laugh.

He looked at his watch and stood up.

His broad frame was taller than I had anticipated and his well-tailored, dark pin-stripe suit gave him an air of elegance. We stood up too. As Kloof guided him towards the lift, Flyte suddenly stopped and turned, addressing me, as if he had suddenly remembered something.

'Mr Roberts — Tony, isn't it? I must thank you for looking after my daughter and her mother so well. They speak very highly of you. I'd like you to have drinks with them and one or two of my friends tomorrow evening — and myself of course. Shall we say about 6.30 at the Dorchester? They're moving into a suite there in the morning. You can make it, can't you?'

Before I had a chance to reply, Lord Kloof said, 'Of course he can, Ray. You'll look forward to it, won't you, Tony?'

I nodded in agreement.

When the doors closed behind Flyte, Lord Kloof came back from the lift. He stood under his portrait and lit a fresh cigar, puffing at it for a time and looking at each of us in turn.

'Right. Listen to what I have to say.

We are not, repeat not, going to run the Flyte scandal exposure, for the simple reason that the informants, if we can call them that, are no longer going to inform, so we have no scandal to expose. I'm sure you'll agree with that Hamish. But even if we had, I'm not sure it would be in our overall best interests to publish, because of the broader issues involved.'

He puffed again on his cigar. I started to say something but he gestured me to be silent.

'There are a variety of factors we have to consider. We don't want any government or City scandal that might bring pressure on the pound. We don't want to rock the boat just when there are signs of growing industrial expansion, more employment and a stable economy. The Flyte-FIG merger will be an example to others. Many of our industrial groups need to rationalise and merge, and the Raymond Flytes of this world show others the way.

'In the last couple of days I've talked to a Cabinet minister, two bank chairmen, the chairman of an insurance company and a major industrialist. I'm quite convinced, as a result, that whatever the circumstances of Flyte's private life and those he associates with, this merger must go through.'

He looked around at all of us.

'I think I've made my position quite clear.' He nodded at myself and Henry and added, 'You two can take yourselves off now. I want to have a talk with Hamish.'

We were dismissed.

* * *

An hour later, I sat in the hotel bar with Pat telling her of the extraordinary events of the day — my conviction that Henry was the informer in our midst, the flight of Maggie Milner, the meeting with Raymond Flyte and the decision and comments of Lord Kloof. We speculated about my invitation for drinks with Jane and her mother. Just what was Flyte up to. This was no idle invitation.

'I've got some news for you, too,' Pat

said rather hesitantly.

'Oh. Good or bad?' I asked.

'I think it's what might be called, inevitable. Particularly when related to the other things that have been happening. I've been advised by my Arab masters to go back to Saudi.'

'How do you mean — advised?' I asked.

I went to see my Saudi contact at the Embassy who looks after the medical side. He explained to me that the Embassy had received information that I had not been solely involved in what I had come home to do. The way he put it was that my stay in the UK had become extended by outside events. He wrapped it all up very politely, but reminded me of my contractual obligation. Someone has obviously put the word in there, and I suspect at a high level. Our friend Flyte, do you think? Anyway, I'm booked to fly out of here next Monday morning. I'll just have to leave things in the hands of the family solicitor, and let him make any final arrangements.'

'By one means or another,' I commented,

'this whole business has suddenly been shut down.'

* * *

Before we went to bed that night it was arranged that Pat should travel down to her home first thing in the morning. I would follow in the evening, once I had been to Flyte's drinks party.

12

A maid answered my ring of the door bell and I stepped into the entrance hall of the plush hotel suite. She handed me a glass of champagne and I turned towards the open double doors that led into the sitting-room. Jane Flyte came through at that moment, glass in hand, and kissed me lightly on the cheek. I don't know which hair stylist she had been to, but someone who knew what they were doing had reshaped her hair, accentuating the fine contours of her face. A beautician had changed her make-up and some expensive fashion house had clothed her slim, neat figure. She had been attractive before. Now she was quite outstanding. She slipped her arm into mine and said quietly:

'Keep your cool and play it calm. We'll talk later.'

We walked into the room beyond, and I saw at the far end Mrs Beryl Flyte and three men wearing dinner-jackets. Raymond Flyte detached himself from the group, came forward with a big smile, and offered an outstretched hand of welcome.

'Delighted to see you, Tony. I'm so glad you could join our gathering. Let me introduce you to the others.'

Jane relinquished her hold on my arm as Flyte led me over.

'Mrs Flyte you know,' he began.

I nodded politely towards her and she smiled back with a firm gaze, almost as if she were trying to pass a silent message to me.

'This is Sir Hugh Laverton.'

I took the outstretched hand of a tall distinguished-looking man with fair hair and military moustache.

'And here we have a visitor from Germany. Herr Wilhelm Muller.'

A short, fat, balding dark-haired man shook hands with me. I felt a lump rising in my throat as I thought of the video tape and the sex scene in Germany Jane had told us about. I was pulled back to the present by Flyte's warm, courteous voice saying:

'Sir Hugh and Herr Muller are co-directors with me of Flyte Enterprises. They will be joining me on the main board of our forthcoming merged company.' By way of expanding the conversation, Flyte added, 'Mr Roberts has recently returned from three years covering the Middle East, is that not correct, Tony?'

'How interesting,' said Muller in his heavily accented English. 'Do you know Bahrein well?'

I told him that I did, and he mentioned some names of government officials that I had briefly met there. Sir Hugh Laverton joined in the conversation and we turned to other Arab countries. We discussed various Middle East developments, both commercial and political. Once or twice I glanced at Flyte who was standing quietly nearby, and I caught the amused smile of those mocking brown eyes of his. Beryl Flyte and Jane joined in the talk, asking me questions about housing, domestic matters, and the place of women in Arab society.

It was as if I knew nothing of past

events and what lay secretly behind the faces of these men. Courtesy, charm and good manners were the order of the day. A casual observer would have thought that this was a typical small social gathering of well-informed, distinguished people. No hint or knowledge of doubtful past activities intruded in any way. This was not the arena for a bare knuckles-contest.

The waitress filled our glasses again and Flyte took me gently by the arm.

'I've got to break up this interesting discussion,' he said. 'I want to talk to Tony for a few minutes. Let's go through into the next room.'

He steered me towards an adjacent door and as he opened it, he turned to Jane and asked her to join us.

We walked through into a dining-room. Flyte motioned me to sit down next to him. Jane took a seat opposite to us, across the table.

Flyte leaned on the table for a moment, his hands clasped in front of him. Then he turned to me and said:

'That went off very well. Let me

compliment you upon your relaxed control in a difficult situation. Very impressive. I like that.'

I puzzled for a moment what to reply, but Flyte continued:

'In case you're wondering, my two colleagues are well aware of what you, and your newspaper, have been up to. I thought, though, that it would finally lay the ghost if we met tonight, in — what shall we say? — friendly accord? You will now see for yourself that any rancour that might have existed between Jane and her mother, and others here tonight, has finally been extinguished. The past is past, and it's the future that we have to look towards. That's right, Jane, isn't it?'

Jane declined to answer her father's rhetorical question but looking at me explained:

'What you have witnessed, Tony, is a beautifully stage-managed closing of the ranks of top Flyte people,' Jane replied. 'On this occasion in private — but there will be public shows too in the future.'

'Don't you think I'm owed an

explanation?' I asked her.

'What it boils down to is that the account is closed,' said Flyte firmly. 'Is it not, Jane?'

Jane nodded.

'You got yourself mixed up in something out of your depth,' Flyte went on. 'You're good. Very good. And you dug up some beautiful dirt, but to be effective you had to be able to use it — and you couldn't. Kloof saw to that.'

I looked again at Jane across the table. 'This doesn't turn your father, or those other two, into shining saints,' I told her. 'What brought about this change of heart?'

'I'll answer that for her,' said Flyte. 'Business. Hard-headed business. To which my ex-wife is no stranger, as I believe you know. Fortunately, too, we seem to have passed this attribute on to Jane here. Whereas she might have despised the concept at one time, she's now come to her senses. Perhaps seeing the realities of life would be a better way of putting it.'

'I suppose you bought them off?' I suggested.

'You could put it that way, but then most people have their price,' he answered.

'Maggie Milner too?' I asked.

He laughed. 'Oh! Maggie. Especially Maggie.'

'Am I going to be told just how?'

Flyte glanced at his watch.

'We men have got to leave for a dinner shortly, and then you'll have a chance to chat with the women. They'll no doubt satisfy your insatiable curiosity. But you'll have seen for yourself that our little group is all friends again, ostensibly anyway. I felt it important that you should witness the scene for yourself.' He paused.

'Now that we have established that situation, there is a proposition I want to put to you. I have taken the trouble to find out about you personally, and what I know is all good. Excellent in fact. I can use someone like you.'

'Do you mean, to use me in the same way as Henry Lust?' I spat.

He smiled again, almost indulgently.

'For heaven's sake, Tony, come down off that high horse of yours for a minute, and listen. No. Not like Lust, but I might add that it further impressed me that you finally tumbled to him. No. I want to offer you a job with me. In the framework of the new head office that I am forming. I need a Press and Publicity Director, and I want you to join me in that capacity.'

'You mean you want to buy my silence too?' I asked peevishly. 'To add me to your little bunch of puppets.'

Flyte banged his hands on the table, stood up with an angry frown on his face, and walked around the table to Jane.

'For God's sake, talk to this man, Jane. Try and get some sense into his thick skull,' he said furiously.

'Listen, Tony,' Jane said, 'you know what happened to me. I am quite prepared to put all that in the past.'

'For a price,' I interjected.

'Not in the way you mean. Agreed, there was great animosity within the family — but don't you see? My father doesn't need to buy your silence, because the whole thing is over. Finished. By chance you've come to his notice at a time when he needs someone to do a particular job — it's just as simple as that. It's luck — sheer bloody luck. Grab the chance he's offering you while you can.'

'I don't believe this is happening,' I said almost wearily. 'I don't know what I expected of tonight, but certainly not this. You mean to say,' I said addressing Flyte, 'that knowing what I do about you and past events, you want to employ me as part of your head-office team — and there are no strings attached?'

He walked around the table, turned the chair beside me, and sat facing me.

'I am offering you this job for two reasons: firstly because you're very good at your job, and secondly, because you're honest, and that's a very difficult attribute to find in this world where most of us live. I know where I stand with you. I've got paid moles up and down Fleet Street — most people in my position have. Henry Lust is only one of them. Look, man, be sensible. You've got to work for somebody, and I can assure you that if you delve into the past of almost anybody at the top in the newspaper world, you'll find things that will make you blush.'

He looked at his watch.

'I'm going to have to leave shortly, but this is what I'm offering you. You'll get a three-year contract at double your present salary. In addition, there is an annual bonus scheme for executives, plus a car and generous expenses. You should jump at this opportunity. I've come a long way, as you well know, but there are still mountains left for me to climb, and I want good men around me. I pay the best and get the best. I want you too.'

As he spoke the persuasive charm of his personality welled out of him. He rose and said: 'I must be going now. Look after him, Jane. Our friend here is a bit bemused at the moment.' He pulled a business-card from his pocket and scribbled on the back. 'Apart from my London office number, here are my two private numbers in town and country. Phone me — and don't take too long to make up your mind.'

13

I sat with Jane and her mother in the sitting-room after Flyte and his two colleagues had left for their dinner engagement. I was offered another drink, but said I would prefer coffee. The waitress brought a tray and when the door closed behind her, it was Mrs Flyte who opened the conversation, in her direct Northern manner.

'You'll be wanting to know what's been going on,' she stated. 'Plenty, I assure you,' she added with a laugh.

I did not feel in the mood to join in her humour.

'You realise that only three days ago you and Jane were determined to destroy Sir Raymond Flyte and his two chums,' I said. 'Something dramatic must have happened to reverse that situation, watching you pals all act together.'

'That's what it may look like on the surface,' replied Mrs Flyte, 'but I can assure you there's no love lost between us. Not with Raymond, or those other two smarmy bastards. No, it's just a question of basic economics, and Jane and I getting what was rightfully due to us.'

'It would help if you told me all that has happened since I last saw you,' I said, the enormity of the situation still hard to accept.

'Yes, that would be the best thing,' replied Mrs Flyte. 'So much has happened since we last talked with you and Pat . . . '

She composed herself in her chair, took a deep breath and began: 'Well, Pat must have told you about our male visitor, and the letter from Raymond informing us that we were to go to his country home and discuss matters with him there. Of course Raymond would never omit saying that it would be in our *financial* interests to do so. You have to remember, Tony, that if the whole, ghastly story concerning Raymond *was* printed, both Jane and I would be the subject of quite considerable speculation.

And, at the end of the day, what would we have achieved? So, complying with the letter, we arrived at Raymond's country estate before lunch. His new wife, thank God, was away. He gave us a hearty welcome, and was friendship and warmth personified. But he could hardly take his eyes off Jane. He was really delighted with the attractive and personable young woman she'd become.

'We got down to serious business after lunch. I won't recount everything we talked about. Let's just say that there was a jockeying for position. What it boiled down to was that he knew all about the newspaper articles and openly admitted that they would harm him. They had got to be stopped, in the national interest as well as our own, and it would be better for all concerned, if we came to an amicable arrangement with him. When we got to that point, I knew it was straightforward horse-trading.

'In the end we did a deal. We didn't get quite as much as I'd planned but we agreed to accept payment in Flyte Enterprise shares from Raymond's own personal holding. I knew they were rising daily on the stock-market and when the new group was formed, and their new shares were traded for old, there would be a further jump in the value. I also liked the idea because it gave Jane and me a stake in the empire I had helped to build.

'I made one extra condition. One that he owed me. I reminded him that had our son lived and developed along the lines he'd originally mapped out for him he would now be well established in the firm. I told him that alternatively, Jane would probably have joined the firm some years ago — if he hadn't treated her so badly. Now was the time to put all that right.

'For a moment he looked puzzled. Then I insisted that Jane be appointed immediately as a director of his companies. I cut short his objections by saying that it could easily be arranged. With his own influence, and that of Laverton and Muller, any resistance could be overcome. No directorships for Jane, I told him and the whole deal was off.

'He didn't answer at first, but got up from his seat and stood looking through the huge stone mullioned window, out over the garden. Then he turned and looked at me and announced enthusiastically that Jane could be his Personal Assistant and how much he liked the idea of his own daughter being on the board.

'I understand that Maggie Milner has been paid off, once and for all, so that there should be no fuss from that quarter. So you see, Tony, once again Raymond seems to have tied up all the loose ends while at the same time keeping his own hands clean.'

I sat for a while quite stupefied by all the events that had taken place. It was quite unbelievable . . . to think I worried about the unprincipled world of the Middle East! There was no comparison with the dealings that seemed to have gone on in the last couple of days.

'And you, Jane, are you happy with all this?' I ventured to ask.

'Yes,' Jane answered. 'I am. As Mother has said, with you and your newspaper I'd have got money — but a lot of hassle too. This way, there's no publicity, more money, a job, directorships which will bring in extra income, a stake in the company and an interesting future. Which choice of the two alternatives would you have made?'

'I know one thing,' I replied sharply. 'I wouldn't have just sold out as you two have done. Christ, I can't believe this. Don't you see that you're in exactly the same league as Maggie Milner and your father, come to that? All that matters is money.'

I was angry, and I sounded angry. Suddenly in the pause in our conversation, I registered the look of alarm on Mrs Flyte's face.

'Good God, Tony,' she said. 'You don't think that this is the end of the matter, do you? I haven't explained things very well to you if that's what you believe. Jane and I have changed our tactics. We pinned our hopes on your newspaper but suddenly the situation altered. As a result, we've won the first round of the revised contest. What we've managed to accomplish, for a start, is to get from

Raymond the financial benefits that were rightfully ours.'

'And what happens next?' I asked.

'I don't know — yet,' replied Mrs Flyte, 'but don't imagine that we've forgotten what Raymond did to Jane, and I haven't forgotten that he was responsible for my son's death. Raymond's a bastard but we have to live with that thought, and turn the new situation to our advantage. There's plenty of time . . . This is just a temporary truce of sorts, brought about by necessity.'

'How can you be sure that Raymond won't tumble to this?' I asked. 'After all, you and everyone else agree that he's an arch manipulator, and a clever man.'

'Believe me, we've fooled him. What you've got to understand is that whereas he knows me, I also know him — very well indeed. Probably better than anyone else can possibly know. That's what I'm playing on now — two of his vulnerable features.'

'What would those be?' I queried.

'His ego and his vanity. He has his many strengths but also has weaknesses and, given time, those weaknesses can be exploited. He's cock-a-hoop at the moment because he's manoeuvred himself out of danger, and the merger will go through. Don't imagine though that I, or Jane, have had a change of heart, because we haven't. But we've won something too.'

'The financial settlement, you mean?'

'No. Not just that. Raymond's really very struck by Jane. He's pleased and proud of her. I've exploited this aspect of his ego and vanity to get her installed at the very heart of the Company. Where that's going to take us, I don't know at the moment. I don't have to remind you about the Trojan Horse, do I? Jane will be playing her part, you can be sure of that, and Raymond will become convinced that he's won her back into his camp. He's a conceited and confident sod — that must be obvious to you, and I know it all too well. Let him think that his magnetic charm has worked on Jane, and let's see how the situation develops. This is only a start. Can't you see what we are doing, Tony?'

When she stopped talking, there was

an absolute silence in the room. I did not know what to reply and I sat there, with both women staring hard at me.

'How can you be sure that he's not just using Jane in one of his devious plans that you haven't yet tumbled to?' I asked finally.

'I can't,' replied Mrs Flyte, 'and there's always that possibility. Jane, though, is now much wiser than she was in the ways of her father and the world. Also, she has me — and hopefully you — to keep an eye on things. You are going to help, aren't you?'

I did not have an answer. What on earth could I say? Events seemed to have moved too swiftly for me. I got to my feet and told them I must catch my train down to Hampshire.

'And what are you going to decide about this job with my father?' Jane asked.

'Decide? I'm far too confused to decide anything at the moment. No offence, but I just want to get the hell out of here.'

14

It was late when I reached Pat's house and I sat at the kitchen table while she cooked bacon and eggs for me. She was intrigued to know what had happened that evening but I found it difficult to put it into coherent words. She listened quietly, interposing with a question here and there. I kept back Flyte's offer of a job to the last. In retrospect, I suppose, even then I was building up a kind of conscience factor about it.

'What did you tell him?' she asked.

'Nothing,' I answered. 'I was too taken aback by it all.'

'I'd have told him to get stuffed,' said Pat.

'It isn't quite as straightforward as you might think,' I replied, and I tried to justify my giving consideration to the offer. Pat listened, but I felt that what I was trying to say was not very well received by her. Finally we went to bed.

We didn't make love that night and it upset me. It was almost as if Pat had withdrawn from me a little. I realised now that I had fallen in love with her and even this small rejection seemed hard to take.

* * *

Over the next few days we hardly spoke about the Flyte affair, almost as if we had tacitly agreed that it had become a taboo subject. Pat and I had a happy time together. We sailed, we walked, ate snack meals in pubs, had dinner with my friends who had first introduced us, and on the Saturday night before Pat was to return to Saudi, she threw a farewell drinks and supper party.

We lay in bed together on the Sunday morning, talking quietly about the party the night before. We had made love that morning and now Pat lay half asleep with her arms wrapped contentedly around me. But our time together was running out . . . I wanted Pat to be a part of my life — the thought of her return to Saudi created a tremendous feeling of loss.

It was then that I raised with her the subject of marriage. Our marriage. She remained so quiet that for a time, I thought she had dozed off to sleep. Then she opened her eyes.

'It wouldn't work, you know. We are two different kinds of people,' she finally said.

'I can't agree with you there,' I replied. 'But what does that matter anyway? Opposites are supposed to attract.'

'I don't mean different in temperament or personality. It's more a question of . . . how shall I put it? How we view things.'

'But we view things in the same way, or I've always thought we did,' I replied.

She suddenly sat up, put a pillow against the headboard, and pulled the sheet over her bare breasts.

'When you were talking to me the other night after you'd met the Flyte entourage, it all hit me suddenly. I realised then, that you and I live and work in two different worlds. You have to go on living in your world, and I want to go on living in mine. I'm a doctor who's interested and happy in my profession.

'I suppose the basis on which all doctors function is helping people. It sounds pompous, but I have a wish to help suffering humanity — or something like that.'

'Well, why is that incompatible with what I do?'

'Your world is pushy, thrusting, dog eat dog, and the devil take the hindmost. My world is an attempt at kindness and a desire to help people. We're poles apart.'

'But surely you can't think that I'm that type? I don't like these things any more than you do, but I accept them as the way things are. Anyway, you were as enthusiastic as I to fix Flyte after what he'd done to your father and then to your mother. God only knows, everyone tried hard enough, but it didn't work — this time. There will no doubt be another chance in the murky scheme of things.'

'That's what I'm trying to say,' she insisted. 'The way things are in your world, not in mine. My dear man, listen to me for a moment and don't let's start scratching at one another. We've had a lovely time together and my eyes have been opened to a lot of things I didn't know before. But I like my job in Saudi where I'm learning things all the time about my speciality, heart disease. Marriage just doesn't enter into my plans yet.'

'What if I changed my job? Would you marry me then?' I asked.

'Oh, Tony, don't be ridiculous. You are as wedded to your job as I am to mine. We are both doing things we are damned good at. In any case, you are going to change your job, aren't you? — or have I read the signs wrong?'

'What's that supposed to mean?' I asked.

She sighed.

'I like you very much, Tony, but sometimes you're very transparent. My bet is that you're secretly pleased about this job Flyte has offered you. You didn't reject it positively at the time. You're teetering on the brink, and trying to

287

make up your mind what you should do. Aren't you?'

I didn't answer for a moment.

'There you are,' she said. 'You *are* thinking about it!'

I started to say something, but she pulled the pillow from behind her head, and pushed it over my face in a playful gesture.

'Let's stop this deep, philosophical discussion,' she said, 'before we spoil our lovely relationship. Let's have a lovely, long, lazy day in bed, and not think about the world outside.'

★ ★ ★

I drove Pat to London Airport the following morning, and we clung to each other when we got to the entrance of the departure lounge. I had suggested that I could arrange to see her on to the plane, but she wanted no lingering farewells.

Holding me close, she suddenly said: 'Listen to me, my darling Tony. I was probably hard on you yesterday when we were talking about what you should do next. I was terribly afraid that we'd spoil our last day together by hours of abstruse discussion. I didn't want that. Only you can decide for yourself what you must do. You're a decent and honest man and maybe someone like you is needed to bring Flyte to book. I realise now that I started off by seeking revenge for what Flyte had done to my parents. It wasn't revenge or restitution that I should have been looking for, but justice. Revenge is a cruel motive. Whether you'll be able to achieve justice, I don't know. If you do then you know where to find me.'

I started to say something but she smothered my words with a kiss and broke away from me. When she turned I caught a glimpse of the tears spilling down her cheeks.

As she got to the barrier, she turned and waved to me, and then she was gone.

I walked slowly through the crowded terminal building and found a section of public telephones. I phoned my office and was put through to Bill Travis.

'How are you fixed for lunch today?' I asked him.

'Quite free — if you're paying,' he answered. 'You sound very far away, where are you?'

'At London Airport,' I replied. 'I've just seen Pat off to Saudi.'

'I suppose you want to cry in your beer?' Bill said.

'Yes, that. And something else I want to talk over with you. What about Simpsons in the Strand — downstairs bar at one o'clock?' I answered.

'Delighted. See you then.'

★ ★ ★

Bill and I had a pint of beer together in the bar and then went up to the dining-room. We talked generally over our meal and it was not until the coffee came that I broached the subject I had on my mind. I brought Bill up to date about my involvement with Flyte and told him about the job offer.

'Christ, man, why are you hesitating?'

he said. 'Jobs like that don't grow on trees.'

'I suppose,' I answered, 'because I'm not sure what I'll be getting myself into. As you know, I'm happy working with you at the newspaper, and I'm not a fanatic about money. I get more than enough for my needs. I even save. I might be moving from a job that I know and like, into something I thoroughly dislike, just for added status and money.'

'You do talk a lot of bollocks sometimes,' Bill said. 'You can save now because you are single and in some respects, a thrifty sod. But you'll marry, most men do, and when you've got a wife and children to support, you'll think differently. Anyway, it was only a short time ago, that we were sitting at almost this very table and you were sounding off about the morality of business practices in the Middle East. Do you remember? I told you to shove off on leave and get yourself sorted out. Now you say you are happy. Go on! Tell me — what's changed?'

'I've been involved in this Flyte business since then,' I answered, 'and

I suppose I've learnt a thing or two.'

'That's what life's all about, isn't it? We all learn something as we go along. At least we should. But, Tony, you've really come to me for advice, haven't you?' He asked, changing the mood. 'Well, I'm going to give you some. If you stay with the newspaper, doing what you are now, you'll undoubtedly end up doing my job or even better, with us or another newspaper along Fleet Street.

'I'm not going to tell you my life story, but it's fairly typical of people in the similar position to me. You've done a stint in the Middle East and now, as things stand, you'll go to Africa next. After that it could be the Far East, perhaps America, Moscow, you name it — in time you'll go all over the world. In abstract, it sounds very interesting, but moving around every few years will play havoc with your personal life.' Bill paused and for a moment was wrapped in his own thoughts.

'Tony,' he continued, 'knowing what I know now, if I'd had your opportunity all those years ago of the job that you've been offered, I'd have grabbed it with both hands. The world's a messy place whether you work for Kloof, Flyte, or a host of other big names. If you don't want to accept that, then get out of our game altogether and open a bookshop or something. Because that's the way things are.'

Bill poured himself another cup of coffee, and tipped in two hefty spoonfuls of sugar.

I said: 'There's one thing I haven't told you, Bill . . . '

Bill suddenly looked up from the vigorous stirring of his coffee. 'Carry on, old boy,' he said with a half smile. 'I think I'm unshockable after the filth you stirred up about Flyte.'

I paused momentarily: in the game, who could you trust? I gambled. 'It's about Henry.'

His eyes flicked up to mine then down again. He listened as I told him how I had unearthed Henry as the mole in our midst. It was an unpleasant discovery. He just nodded when I had finished.

'It figures,' he said, almost without

expression. 'He earns about the same as I do, but I have wondered how he managed to keep up that expensive life-style of his. Thanks for telling me. You haven't told anyone else — Hamish, for example?' he queried.

'No,' I replied, shaking my head.

'Why not?'

'I thought I'd keep it up my sleeve, in case I wanted to use it one day.'

He lifted his head and looked me straight in the eye.

'My God,' he said, 'you're learning, you old bastard.'

He finished his coffee and stood up. He put his hand on my shoulder and said: 'Keep in touch, wherever you may be.'

He walked out of the restaurant, leaving me sitting there.

★ ★ ★

That afternoon I drove to my parents' home. They were pleased to see me. Over the next few days I took long walks in the country, and thought over the whole

294

myriad of recent happenings.

My parents must have noticed my silent preoccupation, but they allowed me to brood on my own. It was on my third night at home that my father suggested that he and I drove out to our favourite country pub. We sat down at our usual table and enjoyed the friendly atmosphere of the place. It was not until we had consumed a couple of pints that my father suddenly said, with a wry twinkle in his eye:

'What's wrong, Tony? Is it this girl you've been seeing?'

I did not answer immediately.

'Only partly,' I replied cautiously. 'It goes very much deeper than that.'

'Why don't you tell me about it? Maybe I can help.'

'I'm not sure that you'd understand,' I replied. 'It's all rather complicated.'

He laughed. 'I'm sure that's the classic remark used by sons to their fathers over the past two thousand years. Parents are people too, you know. Why don't you try me?'

As best I could, I told him the whole

story from beginning to end. I could see from my father's expression throughout this incredible monologue, that father or not, he'd never come across such an amazing story. He remained quite speechless for some time when I had given him the final instalment, shaking his head in mystified disbelief.

'Well,' he said finally, 'it solves one thing. I have often wondered if I did the right thing tucking myself away in a small country bank rather than try and achieve with the high-flyers — but now I'm convinced I did the right thing. Goodness me, I still can't take it all in.' He took a large gulp of his beer. 'Tell me this though, Tony, what was your motive . . . for delving into Flyte's past in the first place. Was it just to please a pretty face, or was it to bring Flyte toppling down?'

'I must admit that it started with the pretty face, as you put it, but as I dug deeper, I became more involved in the justice of the situation.'

'Now the pretty face has gone, at least for the time being, you are thinking of

296

giving up. Is that it? The evil of Flyte will be allowed to continue and you don't do anything about it. Is that what you're proposing?'

'I thought that by taking up this job offer, I might help Jane and Mrs Flyte.'

'These are deep waters you are fishing in,' my father replied, 'and it can get very rough out there at times. What you have to decide for yourself is what is right and what is wrong, and where you stand in relation to both. It's as simple as that. I imagine that it could be the best way of doing things to get up close, and work from inside the organisation. You may be right.'

At the end of the week I phoned Raymond Flyte, and fixed an appointment to see him.

One month later I joined his staff.

15

My move from the world of newspapers into the world of commerce was not such a traumatic experience as I thought it might be. The new head office of Flyfel, as the combined merged companies, were named, occupied the two top floors of a tall office block in the heart of the City. I learned later that the company owned the building, and rented out the lower floors to other organisations. On the top of the block, for all the world to see, large illuminated letters on each side spelt out the name Flyfel.

I was further helped in my transition by being a member of an office team that had been newly formed. Flyte had selected some of his staff from his old office, and added to them by promoting suitably from within the previously existing groups. A few, like myself, had been recruited from outside. The overall result was that, instead of my joining an old, well-established team, I was only one of many who were adjusting to a new scene and environment.

I had an office on the top floor, near to the Chairman's suite, with a larger office next door where I installed the small specialist press and publicity team that was to assist me.

It was of great interest to me to study at close quarters Flyte's style of management, and I could not help but admire it. He would make derisory remarks about other organisations, smaller than ours, but with head offices bulging with staff. Their job in life, he said, was to administer themselves and forget that they had a function outside their own headquarters. Flyte's policy was to delegate responsibility downwards to group individual companies, and allow the man in charge on the spot, within reasonable limits, to have his head and make his own decisions — and not, as he put it, to apply to head office every time they needed to buy a new toilet roll.

Flyte's personal office was large and furnished in a very modern style. A small flat adjoined, in case he needed to stay overnight. A long boardroom and other rooms made up his own personal suite and Jane was there in an office next to his.

It was particularly noticeable to myself, and others, how the relationship between Jane and her father blossomed every day. He obviously adored having her around, and it became a matter of general comment that they seemed to live in each other's pocket.

All the national newspapers were examined daily by one of my staff. Apart from reports we received weekly from a press-cutting agency, general press comments concerning the group or personalities within it were cut out and circulated to the Chairman and other top management. The close relationship between father and daughter itself soon became a matter of press comment. One of the tabloids really did them proud on its front page. The caption in bold print under the photograph read '*TOP AND BOTTOM FLYTE?*'

I showed it to Jane, who was delighted

and chuckled away for some time over it. She asked me not to pass it to her father, as usual, but to have a copy enlarged which she would frame. When she gave it to him, he was so pleased that he added it to his collection of photographs on his office wall. On occasions thereafter he introduced Jane as 'My bottom half' and then added impishly, 'with the accent on the bottom.'

It was about six months after I had joined the organisation that Jane came through to my office one particular morning.

'The master wants you,' she said, 'and he's in one of his foul moods, so be careful. We've all had a slanging from him already about something or other. It's going to be one of those days,' she added with expression.

'What's upset him?' I asked.

'I don't know,' she replied. 'He wants to talk to you about that latest speech you drafted for him — you'd better bring your copy. I've got mine.'

Flyte was standing at the window, looking out over the roof-tops of London, when Jane and I walked into his office. He turned around and scowled at me. Then he walked over to his desk and picked up a sheaf of papers.

'You've got no bloody idea, Tony, of how to put a speech together,' he thundered. 'This latest effort of yours is unadulterated crap.'

'Sir Raymond,' I replied calmly, 'I'm not an experienced speechwriter and have never claimed to be. I do my best. Would you mind telling me what's wrong with it?'

'Wrong! Wrong! It's all bloody wrong,' he shouted back at me aggressively. 'You should know that the conference I shall be addressing . . . '

But he got no further.

Suddenly he stopped in full flow, his face grimaced tightly, his left arm clutched upwards in a knot, and he staggered towards his chair. For a moment he stood there with his eyes closed and then toppled into it.

Jane and I shot a look at one another, then rushed towards him. Flyte's breathing was heavy and he appeared to be unconscious, his left arm posed in a claw.

'Quick,' I said to Jane, 'tell his secretary to phone for an ambulance. I'll get someone to help me carry him to the flat.'

The ambulance was not long in coming. Flyte was lifted onto a stretcher from the bed I had transferred him to. He had regained consciousness by then. 'My arm, my leg,' he said weakly, gazing up at Jane, who went with him in the ambulance as he was rushed off to hospital.

I notified those directors who were in their offices. The Deputy Chairman, Sir Hugh Laverton, was out, but was contacted. I went back to my office and told my staff to put queries through to me personally, and otherwise to make no comment about Flyte and his medical condition. The news would soon be out, and the press and media would be phoning in for information. The afternoon was a hectic one for me and it was about six o'clock when my phone rang yet again. It was Jane.

'How is he?' I asked.

'As well as can be expected, they say. Apparently it's a mild stroke, and we can be thankful for that at least. The doctors say he'll be all right in due course. It looks as though he's burst a small blood vessel in part of his brain, and there's a chance that he may have some impairment to his left arm and left leg. He's in intensive care, of course, but they don't think there's any further danger. But listen, Tony, I can tell you more when you get here. Hugh Laverton is with us and the Press vultures have gathered outside. Hugh wants you down here to deal with them.'

'Right, I'm on my way. What about Lady Flyte? Has she been notified?'

'Dear Felicity is out and about, and can't be found,' Jane said with heavy sarcasm. 'Don't worry, she'll no doubt turn up for the benefit of the photographers.'

Her father's second wife was not much loved by his daughter. A week later Flyte was on his feet for the first time and a week after that, was allowed home. He had been warned to rest for a further fortnight before even considering going back to his office, but that was not his way.

A month after his stroke he returned to the office, frustrated by his limp left leg and arm but otherwise as energetic and dynamic as ever. The doctors warned him not to overstretch himself, but he just took his pills and growled.

★ ★ ★

Some months later, I was working late one evening in an attempt to clear my desk. Jane came into my office, poured herself a drink from my cabinet and sat down. She remained quiet until finally I threw the last piece of paper to one side and leant back, easing my aching body.

'Thank God it's Friday,' I remarked. 'What are you up to this weekend?'

'Tomorrow I'm going to stay with friends in the country. But tonight I'm at a loose end. How about you and I having dinner together?'

'That sounds a great idea,' I answered.

'I missed lunch and I'm starving.'

We took my car to a restaurant in Belgravia, had a couple of drinks at the bar, and chatted happily together over our meal. A long table had been prepared at the far end of the room for a party that was yet to arrive. We observed them with amused curiosity when they did come in — six smart men and six elegant women, talking loudly among themselves. One of the women was clutching the arm of a tall, ruddy-faced man. He said something to her and she threw back her head and laughed raucously. At that moment I recognised her. It was Lady Flyte.

'Fucking Felicity,' Jane observed irreverently.

At that moment, Felicity turned and saw us. She tugged on the arm of her escort and they made their way along the restaurant towards us.

'What a happy scene,' she remarked merrily. 'May I introduce Harry Holmes? He breeds racehorses — among other things.' She giggled. 'Do you know who this is, Harry?' she asked, looking at Jane.

'Would you believe it, she's my step-daughter and only a few years younger than me?'

She whispered something into her escort's ear. His eyes darted at Jane, knowingly.

'How very interesting,' he remarked with a smirk. 'In that case we must very definitely meet again.' Together they giggled as they walked back to rejoin their party.

Jane's face was a blank dark mask.

'Bitch,' was all she remarked, and went on eating. We were silent for a time — the intrusion having removed the relaxed atmosphere that had existed between us.

'I've often wondered how you got on with your step-mother,' I ventured.

'The simple answer is that we don't,' she replied.

'I rather gathered that. Does she play around much?' I asked cautiously.

'Far too much for my father's taste. But he realises that there's a large age-gap between them, and to put it in her horsey language, he allows her a free rein — up to a point. On some matters, though, there are definite restrictions.'

She put her knife and fork down neatly on her plate and went on:

'You see. Daddy is very anxious to get his peerage one day, and Felicity's father has some pull in that quarter. When he married Felicity, Daddy provided money that her family urgently needed. In fact he holds a mortgage on her family property, so her father has good financial reasons for keeping Daddy sweet. In the meantime, he's got a young glamorous wife that he's added to his collection of assets — if you can call her that.' She thrust her napkin down on the table. 'Come on, Tony. That bitch over there is ruining our evening. Let's go back to my place for a drink.'

16

Jane had a small flat in a quiet mews off Eaton Place. When we arrived there, we sat at the small bar that had been tastefully constructed in an alcove to one side of the drawing-room. Behind the bar, she lifted a bottle of champagne out of a refrigerator, and handed it to me. As I was removing the foil and unscrewing the wire, she leaned on the bar top, looking at me, her face cupped in her hands.

'Do you like my father,' she suddenly asked.

'Like is not a word I would use,' I replied. 'Respect, yes. Admire in some contexts, yes. But I don't think he's a man you like. At least, not the way you mean it.'

'You've changed a lot, you know?' she said. 'Daddy and I have remarked on it. You've got far more sparkle now than you used to have. You used to be a bit solemn.'

'Well, a lot's happened in the last year, hasn't it?' I replied.

'God. Is it a year?' she enquired.

'It will be,' I replied. 'Next Thursday will be one calendar year since I joined the firm.'

As I was pouring the champagne, she fumbled in her handbag, brought out her diary, and flicked through the pages.

'That's great,' she said finally. 'Next Thursday, you, Daddy and I, just the three of us, will have dinner together to celebrate.'

We sipped our champagne, looking at each other.

'You're a very lucky man,' she said almost cheekily.

'Yes,' I replied, 'I suppose I am. I couldn't have foreseen a year or so ago, what was going to happen.'

'I don't mean lucky like that,' she chuckled.

'How then?'

'Lucky because tonight you're going to screw the boss's daughter. And,' she added with a mischievous grin, 'if you

310

don't make a good job of it — I'll have your balls for earrings.'

★ ★ ★

Our work the following week brought Jane and me into close contact, but no mention was made of our torrid and athletic night in bed together.

She came into my office on the Thursday morning and reminded me of our dinner date with her father that night.

'Quite informal,' she added. 'No dressing up or anything like that. Come round at 7.30 and we'll eat at 8.00. When Daddy's in London he likes to watch the ten o'clock news on television. Straight after that, he goes to bed. I wouldn't want to break his routine. His doctors are still going on about how he should rest, and not get over-excited.'

We had a pleasant dinner together. In the drawing room, a maid brought in a tray of coffee. I poured a brandy for each of us. Flyte sat in a large armchair and sipped his drink. At a few minutes to ten, Jane went over to the television and turned it on, with the sound switched off, but the picture showing. At ten o'clock when the news came on, she pressed a button on the remote-control unit to the side of her chair to turn up the sound, and we watched and listened to the first half of the night's news.

Then came the advertising break, and Flyte and I were commenting on some matter of interest we had heard, when Jane got up and walked across to the set. I assumed the sudden silence was because she had turned off the sound during the commercial break.

One moment Flyte was talking to me, the next his eyes had swung back to the screen, and he was staring intently. His good arm went out in a gesture and his whole body froze.

I looked at the screen and for a moment I didn't register what I was seeing. I thought it was another commercial. Then I recognised Felicity — Lady Flyte. She walked elegantly across a bedroom, fully clothed. Beside her were two men, one being the man I had seen with her in the restaurant. They both started embracing her and she responded passionately. The men slowly undid her clothes and slipped them off her onto the floor. They slid down her brief panties, and she stepped out of them. One of them unclipped her bra and drew it from her. When she was naked, they embraced her again. She broke away playfully, pirouetted about the room, and then spread herself seductively across the bed. The two men, now also naked, joined her.

I looked up quickly at Jane who stood at one side of the television set. She was looking hard at Flyte, a faint smile on her face.

'What is this?' Flyte shouted. 'How did this come about? Turn it off, Jane.'

'No, dear father,' she replied quietly. 'You're going to watch your dear wife Felicity enjoying herself.'

The video film showed the three of them on the bed, performing a variety of sexual gyrations. Felicity was the star performer.

Flyte again shouted: 'Turn that damned thing off. Turn it off, do you hear me?'

He tried to lift himself out of his chair, and I too rose from my seat. The film went on running and a gargled cry rang out from Flyte as he again tried to rise.

Suddenly he cried out again, his body convulsed, and he fell back into his chair. His gaze was fixed on the television screen and the film that ran on remorselessly. Finally his eyes closed, and with a groan, he slumped into unconsciousness.

I rushed over to him, and tried to lift him up. He was breathing, but otherwise there was no movement from him. In place of the famous Flyte smile, there had appeared on his face a drawn, twisted mask. Saliva oozed from his open mouth, across his chin, and dribbled onto his chest.

'My God,' I said to Jane. 'What have you done?'

She was still standing there with that half smile on her face.

She switched off the video machine, ejected the tape, and held it up in her hand before slipping it into her handbag.

'A trick I learnt from my dear father,' she said. 'Only this time, the camera was concealed. In this case I think the appropriate expression is 'Like father — like daughter'.'

'But why?' I asked. 'For God's sake, why?'

She walked over and looked down at her unconscious father. I was struck again at that moment by the family resemblance to Raymond Flyte — as he had once been.

I went over to the telephone and dialled for an emergency ambulance.

I removed Flyte's shoes, then loosened his tie. Within five minutes I could hear the sound of a siren heading in our direction.

'Don't worry,' said Jane calmly. 'Knowing him, he won't die — he'll hang on. But he'll just become a totally incapacitated cabbage. The doctors will call it a massive stroke — from overwork.'

She picked up her brandy glass, raised it in a toast to her father, then laughed.

'What the hell is there to laugh about?' I asked curtly.

'It was a joke of Father's that used to amuse him. He used to say that whenever there's a marriage, someone is bound to get fucked. This time, it's him.'

THE END

We do hope that you have enjoyed reading this large print book.

Did you know that all of our titles are available for purchase?

We publish a wide range of high quality large print books including:
Romances, Mysteries, Classics, General Fiction, Non Fiction and Westerns.

Special interest titles available in large print are:
The Little Oxford Dictionary Music Book, Song Book Hymn Book, Service Book

Also available from us courtesy of Oxford University Press:
Young Readers' Dictionary (large print edition) Young Readers' Thesaurus (large print edition)

For further information or a free brochure, please contact us at:
Ulverscroft Large Print Books Ltd., The Green, Bradgate Road, Anstey, Leicester, LE7 7FU, England.
Tel: (00 44) **0116 236 4325**
Fax: (00 44) **0116 234 0205**

SIDEWINDER

Jane Morell

Lisette, a British agent sent to the Lebanon to extricate an American hostage, disappears without trace, leaving behind a husband and a young son, Robert. Ten years later, Robert tracks down her betrayer, intent on revenge. Winton, the man responsible, has made a new life for himself in Wales. However, Robert doesn't count on meeting Winton's daughter, Sara. How can he murder the father of the girl he has come to love? But is Sara the innocent creature she appears to be?

SHERLOCK HOLMES AND THE GREYFRIARS SCHOOL MYSTERY

Val Andrews

The senior master has lost the manuscript of the history of the famous Greyfriars School, whose pupils include the overweight schoolboy Billy Bunter. The headmaster calls in old boy Dr Watson and seeks his influence to engage Sherlock Holmes to solve the mystery. The master detective not only traces the missing manuscript but is able to solve a number of other related puzzles — including a murder case — for the local constabulary.